THE CASUARINA TREE

Of the Casuarina tree they say that if you take in a boat with you a piece of it, be it never so small, contrary winds will arise to impede your journey or storms to imperil your life. They say also that if you stand in its shadow by the light of the full moon you will hear, whispered mysteriously in its dark ravage, the secrets of the future. These facts have never been disputed; but they say also that when in the wide estuaries the mangrove has in due time reclaimed the swampy land from the water the Casuarina tree plants itself and in its turn settles, solidifies and fertilises the soil till it is ripe for a more varied and luxuriant growth; and then, having done its work, dies down before the ruthless encroachment of the myriad denizens of the jungle. It occurred to me that The Casuarina Tree would make not so bad a title for a collection of stories about the English people who live in the Malay Peninsula and in Borneo; for I fancied that they, coming after the pioneers who had opened these lands to Western civilisation, were destined in just such a manner, now that their work was accomplished and the country was peaceable, orderly and sophisticated, to give way to a more varied, but less adventurous, generation;

and I was excessively disconcerted on enquiry to learn that there was not a word of truth in what I had been told. It is very hard to find a title for a volume of short stories; to give it the name of the first is to evade the difficulty and deceives the purchaser into thinking that he is about to read a novel; a good title should, however vaguely, have a reference to all the stories gathered together; the best titles have already been used. I was in a quandary. But I reflected that a symbol (as Master Francis Rabelais pointed out in a diverting chapter) can symbolise anything; and I remembered that the Casuarina tree stood along the seashore, gaunt and rough-hewn, protecting the land from the fury of the winds, and so might aptly suggest these planters and administrators who with all their shortcomings have after all brought to the peoples among whom they dwell tranquillity, justice and welfare, and I fancied that they too, as they looked at the Casuarina tree, grey, rugged and sad, a little out of place in the wanton tropics, might very well be reminded of their native land; and, thinking for a moment of the heather on a Yorkshire moor or the broom on a Sussex common, see in that hardy tree, doing its best in difficult circumstances, a symbol of their own exiled lives. In short I could find a dozen reasons for keeping my title, but of course the best of them all was that I could think of no better.

W. S. M.

CONTENTS

BEFORE THE PARTY

BEFORE THE PARTY

MRS. SKINNER liked to be in good time. She was already dressed, in black silk as befitted her age and the mourning she wore for her son-in-law, and now she put on her toque. She was a little uncertain about it, since the egrets' feathers which adorned it might very well arouse in some of the friends she would certainly meet at the party acid expostulations; and of course it was shocking to kill those beautiful white birds, in the mating season too, for the sake of their feathers; but there they were, so pretty and stylish, and it would have been silly to refuse them, and it would have hurt her son-in-law's feelings. He had brought them all the way from Borneo and he expected her to be so pleased with them. Kathleen had made herself rather unpleasant about them, she must wish she hadn't now, after what had happened, but Kathleen had never really liked Harold. Mrs. Skinner, standing at her dressing-table, placed the toque on her head, it was after all the only nice hat she had, and put in a pin with a large jet knob. If anybody spoke to her about the ospreys she had her answer.

"I know it's dreadful," she would say, "and I wouldn't dream of buying them, but my poor son-in-law brought them back the last time he was home on leave."

That would explain her possession of them and excuse their use. Every one had been very kind. Mrs. Skinner took a clean handkerchief from a drawer and sprinkled a little *Eau de Cologne* on it. She never used scent, and she had always thought it rather fast, but *Eau de Cologne* was so refreshing. She was very nearly ready now and her eyes wandered out of the window behind her looking-glass. Canon Heywood had a beautiful day for his garden-party. It was warm and the sky was blue; the trees had not yet lost the fresh green of the spring. She smiled as she saw her little granddaughter in the strip of garden behind the house busily raking her very own flower-bed. Mrs. Skinner wished Joan were not quite so pale, it was a mistake to have kept her so long in the tropics; and she was so grave for her age, you never saw her run about; she played quiet games of her own invention and watered her garden. Mrs. Skinner gave the front of her dress a little pat, took up her gloves, and went down-stairs.

Kathleen was at the writing-table in the window busy with lists she was making, for she was honorary secretary of the Ladies' Golf Club and when there were competitions had a good deal to do. But she too was ready for the party.

"I see you've put on your jumper after all," said Mrs. Skinner.

They had discussed at luncheon whether Kathleen should wear her jumper or her black chiffon. The jumper was black and white, and Kathleen thought it rather smart, but it was hardly mourning. Millicent, however, was in favour of it.

"There's no reason why we should all look as if we'd just come from a funeral," she said. "Harold's been dead eight months."

To Mrs. Skinner it seemed rather unfeeling to talk like that. Millicent was strange since her return from Borneo.

"You're not going to leave off your weeds yet, darling?" she asked.

Millicent did not give a direct answer.

"People don't wear mourning in the way they used," she said. She paused a little and when she went on there was a tone in her voice which Mrs. Skinner thought quite peculiar. It was plain that Kathleen noticed it too, for she gave her sister a curious look. "I'm sure Harold wouldn't wish me to wear mourning for him indefinitely."

"I dressed early because I wanted to say something to Millicent," said Kathleen in reply to her mother's observation.

"Oh?"

Kathleen did not explain. But she put her lists aside and with knitted brows read for the second time a letter from a lady who complained that the committee had most unfairly marked down her handicap from twenty-four to eighteen. It requires a good deal of tact to be Honorary Secretary to a ladies' golf club. Mrs. Skinner began to put on her new gloves. The sun-blinds kept the room cool and dark. She looked at the great wooden hornbill, gaily painted, which Harold had left in her safe-keeping; and it seemed a little odd and barbaric to her, but he had set much store on it. It had some religious significance and Canon Heywood had been greatly struck by it. On the wall, over the sofa, were Malay weapons, she forgot what they were called, and here and there on occasional tables pieces of silver and brass which Harold at various times had sent to them. She had liked Harold and involuntarily her eyes sought his photograph which stood on the piano with photographs of her two daughters, her grandchild, her sister and her sister's son.

"Why, Kathleen, where's Harold's photograph?" she asked.

Kathleen looked round. It no longer stood in its place.

"Some one's taken it away," said Kathleen.

Surprised and puzzled, she got up and went over to the piano. The photographs had been rearranged so that no gap should show.

"Perhaps Millicent wanted to have it in her bed-room," said Mrs. Skinner.

"I should have noticed it. Besides, Millicent has several photographs of Harold. She keeps them locked up."

Mrs. Skinner had thought it very peculiar that her daughter should have no photographs of Harold in her room. Indeed she had spoken of it once, but Millicent had made no reply. Millicent had been strangely silent since she came back from Borneo, and had not encouraged the sympathy Mrs. Skinner would have been so willing to show her. She seemed unwilling to speak of her great loss. Sorrow took people in different ways. Her husband had said the best thing was to leave her alone. The thought of him turned her ideas to the party they were going to.

"Father asked if I thought he ought to wear a top-hat," she said. "I said I thought it was just as well to be on the safe side."

It was going to be quite a grand affair. They were having ices, strawberry and vanilla, from Boddy, the confectioner, but the Heywoods were making the iced coffee at home. Every one would be there. They had been asked to meet the Bishop of Hong-Kong, who was staying with the Canon, an old college friend of his, and he was going to speak on the Chinese missions. Mrs. Skinner, whose daughter had lived in the East for eight years and whose son-in-law had been Resident of a district in Borneo, was in a flutter of interest. Naturally it meant more to her than to people who had never had anything to do with the Colonies and that sort of thing.

"What can they know of England who only England know?" as Mr. Skinner said.

He came into the room at that moment. He was a lawyer, as his father had been before him, and he had offices in Lincoln's Inn Fields. He went up to London every morning and came down every evening. He was only able to accompany his wife **and** daughters to the Canon's garden-party because the

Canon had very wisely chosen a Saturday to have it on. Mr. Skinner looked very well in his tail-coat and pepper-and-salt trousers. He was not exactly dressy, but he was neat. He looked like a respectable family solicitor, which indeed he was; his firm never touched work that was not perfectly above board, and if a client went to him with some trouble that was not quite nice, Mr. Skinner would look grave.

"I don't think this is the sort of case that we very much care to undertake," he said. "I think you'd do better to go elsewhere."

He drew towards him his writing-block and scribbled a name and address on it. He tore off a sheet of paper and handed it to his client.

"If I were you I think I would go and see these people. If you mention my name I believe they'll do anything they can for you."

Mr. Skinner was clean-shaven and very bald. His pale lips were tight and thin, but his blue eyes were shy. He had no colour in his cheeks and his face was much lined.

"I see you've put on your new trousers," said Mrs. Skinner.

"I thought it would be a good opportunity," he answered. "I was wondering if I should wear a buttonhole."

"I wouldn't, father," said Kathleen. "I don't think it's awfully good form."

"A lot of people will be wearing them," said Mrs. Skinner.

"Only clerks and people like that," said Kathleen.

"The Heywoods have had to ask everybody, you know. And besides, we are in mourning."

"I wonder if there'll be a collection after the Bishop's address," said Mr. Skinner.

"I should hardly think so," said Mrs. Skinner.

"I think it would be rather bad form," agreed Kathleen.

"It's as well to be on the safe side," said Mr. Skinner. "I'll give for all of us. I was wondering if ten shillings would be enough or if I must give a pound."

"If you give anything I think you ought to give a pound, father," said Kathleen.

"I'll see when the time comes. I don't want to give less than any one else, but on the other hand I see no reason to give more than I need."

Kathleen put away her papers in the drawer of the writing-table and stood up. She looked at her wrist-watch.

"Is Millicent ready?" asked Mrs. Skinner.

"There's plenty of time. We're only asked at four and I don't think we ought to arrive much before half-past. I told Davis to bring the car round at four-fifteen."

Generally Kathleen drove the car, but on grand occasions like this Davis, who was the gardener, put on his uniform and acted as chauffeur. It looked better when you drove up and naturally Kathleen didn't much want to drive herself when she was wearing her new jumper. The sight of her mother forcing her fingers one by one into her new gloves reminded her that she must put on her own. She smelt them to see if any odour of the cleaning still clung to them. It was very slight. She didn't believe any one would notice.

At last the door opened and Millicent came in. She wore her widow's weeds. Mrs. Skinner never could get used to them, but of course she knew that Millicent must wear them for a year. It was a pity they didn't suit her; they suited some people. She had tried on Millicent's bonnet once, with its white band and long veil, and thought she looked very well in it. Of course she hoped dear Alfred would survive her, but if he didn't she would never go out of weeds. Queen Victoria never had. It was different for Millicent; Millicent was a much younger woman; she was only thirty-six; it was very sad to be a widow at thirty-six. And there wasn't much chance of her marrying again. Kathleen wasn't very likely to marry now, she was thirty-five; last time Millicent and Harold had come home she had suggested that they should have Kathleen to stay with them; Harold had seemed willing enough, but Millicent said it wouldn't do. Mrs. Skinner didn't know why not. It would give her a chance. Of course they didn't want to get rid of her, but a girl ought to marry, and somehow all the men they knew at home were married already. Millicent said the climate was trying. It was true she was a bad colour. No one would think now that Millicent had been the prettier of the two. Kathleen had fined down as she grew older (of course some people said she was too thin) but now that she had cut her hair, with her cheeks red from playing golf in

all weathers, Mrs. Skinner thought her quite pretty.
No one could say that of poor Millicent; she had
lost her figure completely; she had never been tall
and now that she had filled out she looked stocky.
She was a good deal too fat; Mrs. Skinner supposed it was due to the tropical heat that prevented
her from taking exercise. Her skin was sallow
and muddy; and her blue eyes, which had been her
best feature, had gone quite pale.

"She ought to do something about her neck," Mrs.
Skinner reflected. "She's becoming dreadfully
jowly."

She had spoken of it once or twice to her husband.
He remarked that Millicent wasn't as young as she
was: that might be, but she needn't let herself go
altogether. Mrs. Skinner made up her mind to talk
to her daughter seriously, but of course she must
respect her grief and she would wait till the year
was up. She was just as glad to have this reason
to put off a conversation the thought of which made
her slightly nervous. For Millicent was certainly
changed. There was something sullen in her face
which made her mother not quite at home with her.
Mrs. Skinner liked to say aloud all the thoughts
that passed through her head, but Millicent when
you made a remark (just to say something, you
know) had an awkward habit of not answering so
that you wondered whether she had heard. Sometimes Mrs. Skinner found it so irritating, that not
to be quite sharp with Millicent she had to remind
herself that poor Harold had only been dead eight
months.

The light from the window fell on the widow's heavy face as she advanced silently, but Kathleen stood with her back to it. She watched her sister for a moment.

"Millicent, there's something I want to say to you," she said. "I was playing golf with Gladys Heywood this morning."

"Did you beat her?" asked Millicent.

Gladys Heywood was the Canon's only unmarried daughter.

"She told me something about you which I think you ought to know."

Millicent's eyes passed beyond her sister to the little girl watering flowers in the garden.

"Have you told Annie to give Joan her tea in the kitchen, mother?" she said.

"Yes, she'll have it when the servants have theirs."

Kathleen looked at her sister coolly.

"The Bishop spent two or three days at Singapore on his way home," she went on. "He's very fond of travelling. He's been to Borneo and he knows a good many of the people that you know."

"He'll be interested to see you, dear," said Mrs. Skinner. "Did he know poor Harold?"

"Yes, he met him at Kuala Solor. He remembers him very well. He says he was shocked to hear of his death."

Millicent sat down and began to put on her black gloves. It seemed strange to Mrs. Skinner that she received these remarks with complete silence.

"Oh, Millicent," she said, "Harold's photo has disappeared. Have you taken it?"

"Yes, I put it away."

"I should have thought you'd like to have it out."

Once more Millicent said nothing. It really was an exasperating habit.

Kathleen turned slightly in order to face her sister.

"Millicent, why did you tell us that Harold died of fever?"

The widow made no gesture, she looked at Kathleen with steady eyes, but her sallow skin darkened with a flush. She did not reply.

"What *do* you mean, Kathleen?" asked Mr. Skinner, with surprise.

"The Bishop says that Harold committed suicide."

Mrs. Skinner gave a startled cry, but her husband put out a deprecating hand.

"Is it true, Millicent?"

"It is."

"But why didn't you tell us?"

Millicent paused for an instant. She fingered idly a piece of Brunei brass which stood on the table by her side. That too had been a present from Harold.

"I thought it better for Joan that her father should be thought to have died of fever. I didn't want her to know anything about it."

"You've put us in an awfully awkward position," said Kathleen, frowning a little. "Gladys Heywood said she thought it rather nasty of me not to have told her the truth. I had the greatest difficulty in getting her to believe that I knew absolutely nothing about it. She said her father was rather put out.

He says, after all the years we've known one another, and considering that he married you, and the terms we've been on, and all that, he does think we might have had confidence in him. And at all events if we didn't want to tell him the truth we needn't have told him a lie."

"I must say I sympathise with him there," said Mr. Skinner acidly.

"Of course I told Gladys that we weren't to blame. We only told them what you told us."

"I hope it didn't put you off your game," said Millicent.

"Really, my dear, I think that is a most improper observation," exclaimed her father.

He rose from his chair, walked over to the empty fireplace, and from force of habit stood in front of it with parted coat-tails.

"It was my business," said Millicent, "and if I chose to keep it to myself I didn't see why I shouldn't."

"It doesn't look as if you had any affection for your mother if you didn't even tell her," said Mrs. Skinner.

Millicent shrugged her shoulders.

"You might have known it was bound to come out," said Kathleen.

"Why? I didn't expect that two gossiping old parsons would have nothing else to talk about than me."

"When the Bishop said he'd been to Borneo it's only natural that the Heywoods should ask him if he knew you and Harold."

"All that's neither here nor there," said Mr. Skinner. "I think you should certainly have told us the truth and we could have decided what was the best thing to do. As a solicitor I can tell you that in the long run it only makes things worse if you attempt to hide them."

"Poor Harold," said Mrs. Skinner, and the tears began to trickle down her raddled cheeks. "It seems dreadful. He was always a good son-in-law to me. Whatever induced him to do such a dreadful thing?"

"The climate."

"I think you'd better give us all the facts, Millicent," said her father.

"Kathleen will tell you."

Kathleen hesitated. What she had to say really was rather dreadful. It seemed terrible that such things should happen to a family like theirs.

"The Bishop says he cut his throat."

Mrs. Skinner gasped and she went impulsively up to her bereaved daughter. She wanted to fold her in her arms.

"My poor child," she sobbed.

But Millicent withdrew herself.

"Please don't fuss me, mother. I really can't stand being mauled about."

"Really, Millicent," said Mr. Skinner, with a frown.

He did not think she was behaving very nicely.

Mrs. Skinner dabbed her eyes carefully with her handkerchief and with a sigh and a little shake of the head returned to her chair. Kathleen fidgeted with the long chain she wore round her neck.

"It does seem rather absurd that I should have to be told the details of my brother-in-law's death by a friend. It makes us all look such fools. The Bishop wants very much to see you, Millicent; he wants to tell you how much he feels for you." She paused, but Millicent did not speak. "He says that Millicent had been away with Joan and when she came back she found poor Harold lying dead on his bed."

"It must have been a great shock," said Mr. Skinner.

Mrs. Skinner began to cry again, but Kathleen put her hand gently on her shoulder.

"Don't cry, mother," she said. "It'll make your eyes red and people will think it so funny."

They were all silent while Mrs. Skinner, drying her eyes, made a successful effort to control herself. It seemed very strange to her that at this very moment she should be wearing in her toque the ospreys that poor Harold had given her.

"There's something else I ought to tell you," said Kathleen.

Millicent looked at her sister again, without haste, and her eyes were steady, but watchful. She had the look of a person who is waiting for a sound which he is afraid of missing.

"I don't want to say anything to wound you, dear," Kathleen went on, "but there's something else and I think you ought to know it. The Bishop says that Harold drank."

"Oh, my dear, how dreadful!" cried Mrs. Skinner. "What a shocking thing to say. Did Gladys Heywood tell you? What did you say?"

"I said it was entirely untrue."

"This is what comes of making secrets of things," said Mr. Skinner irritably. "It's always the same. If you try and hush a thing up all sorts of rumours get about which are ten times worse than the truth."

"They told the Bishop in Singapore that Harold had killed himself while he was suffering from *delirium tremens*. I think for all our sakes you ought to deny that, Millicent."

"It's such a dreadful thing to have said about any one who's dead," said Mrs. Skinner. "And it'll be so bad for Joan when she grows up."

"But what is the foundation of this story, Millicent?" asked her father. "Harold was always very abstemious."

"Here," said the widow.

"Did he drink?"

"Like a fish."

The answer was so unexpected, and the tone so sardonic, that all three of them were startled.

"Millicent, how can you talk like that of your husband when he's dead?" cried her mother, clasping her neatly gloved hands. "I can't understand you. You've been so strange since you came back. I could never have believed that a girl of mine could take her husband's death like that."

"Never mind about that, mother," said Mr. Skinner. "We can go into all that later."

He walked to the window and looked out at the sunny little garden, and then walked back into the room. He took his pince-nez out of his pocket and, though he had no intention of putting them on, wiped them with his handkerchief. Millicent looked at him and in her eyes, unmistakably, was a look of irony which was quite cynical. Mr. Skinner was vexed. He had finished his week's work and he was a free man till Monday morning. Though he had told his wife that this garden-party was a great nuisance and he would much sooner have tea quietly in his own garden, he had been looking forward to it. He did not care very much about Chinese missions, but it would be interesting to meet the Bishop. And now this! It was not the kind of thing he cared to be mixed up in; it was most unpleasant to be told on a sudden that his son-in-law was a drunkard and a suicide. Millicent was thoughtfully smoothing her white cuffs. Her coolness irritated him; but instead of addressing her he spoke to his younger daughter.

"Why don't you sit down, Kathleen? Surely there are plenty of chairs in the room."

Kathleen drew forward a chair and without a word seated herself. Mr. Skinner stopped in front of Millicent and faced her.

"Of course I see why you told us Harold had died of fever. I think it was a mistake, because that sort of thing is bound to come out sooner or later. I don't know how far what the Bishop has told the Heywoods coincides with the facts, but if you will take my advice you will tell us everything as circumstantially as you can, then we can see. We can't hope that it will go no further now that Canon Heywood and Gladys know. In a place like this people are bound to talk. It will make it easier for all of us if we at all events know the exact truth."

Mrs. Skinner and Kathleen thought he put the matter very well. They waited for Millicent's reply. She had listened with an impassive face; that sudden flush had disappeared and it was once more, as usual, pasty and sallow.

"I don't think you'll much like the truth if I tell it you," she said.

"You must know that you can count on our sympathy and understanding," said Kathleen gravely.

Millicent gave her a glance and the shadow of a smile flickered across her set mouth. She looked slowly at the three of them. Mrs. Skinner had an uneasy impression that she looked at them as though they were mannequins at a dressmaker's. She seemed to live in a different world from theirs and to have no connection with them.

"You know, I wasn't in love with Harold when I married him," she said reflectively.

Mrs. Skinner was on the point of making an exclamation when a rapid gesture of her husband, barely indicated, but after so many years of married life perfectly significant, stopped her. Millicent went on. She spoke with a level voice, slowly, and there was little change of expression in her tone.

"I was twenty-seven, and no one else seemed to want to marry me. It's true he was forty-four, and it seemed rather old, but he had a very good position, hadn't he? I wasn't likely to get a better chance."

Mrs. Skinner felt inclined to cry again, but she remembered the party.

"Of course I see now why y u took his photograph away," she said dolefully

"Don't, mother," exclaimed Kathleen.

It had been taken when he was engaged to Millicent and was a very good photograph of Harold.
Mrs. Skinner had always thought him quite a fine
man. He was heavily built, tall and perhaps a little
too fat, but he held himself well, and his presence
was imposing. He was inclined to be bald, even
then, but men did go bald very early nowadays, and
he said that topees, sun-helmets, you know, were
very bad for the hair. He had a small dark moustache and his face was deeply burned by the sun. Of
course his best feature was his eyes; they were brown
and large, like Joan's. His conversation was interesting. Kathleen said he was pompous, but Mrs.
Skinner didn't think him so, she didn't mind it if a
man laid down the law; and when she saw, as she
very soon did, that he was attracted by Millicent she
began to like him very much. He was always very
attentive to Mrs. Skinner and she listened as though
she were really interested when he spoke of his district and told her of the big game he had killed.
Kathleen said he had a pretty good opinion of himself, but Mrs. Skinner came of a generation which
accepted without question the good opinion that men
had of themselves. Millicent saw very soon which
way the wind blew and, though she said nothing to
her mother, her mother knew that if Harold asked
her she was going to accept him.

Harold was staying with some people who had
been thirty years in Borneo and they spoke well of

the country. There was no reason why a woman shouldn't live there comfortably; of course the children had to come home when they were seven; but Mrs. Skinner thought it unnecessary to trouble about that yet. She asked Harold to dine and she told him they were always in to tea. He seemed to be at a loose end and when his visit to his old friends was drawing to a close she told him they would be very much pleased if he would come and spend a fortnight with them. It was towards the end of this that Harold and Millicent became engaged. They had a very pretty wedding, they went to Venice for their honeymoon, and then they started for the East. Millicent wrote from the various ports at which the ship touched. She seemed happy.

"People were very nice to me at Kuala Solor," she said. Kuala Solor was the chief town of the state of Sembulu. "We stayed with the Resident and every one asked us to dinner. Once or twice I heard men ask Harold to have a drink but he refused; he said he had turned over a new leaf now he was a married man. I didn't know why they laughed. Mrs. Gray, the Resident's wife, told me they were all so glad Harold was married. She said it was dreadfully lonely for a bachelor on one of the out-stations. When we left Kuala Solor Mrs. Gray said good-bye to me so funnily that I was quite surprised. It was as if she was solemnly putting Harold in my charge."

They listened to her in silence. Kathleen never took her eyes off her sister's impassive face, but Mr. Skinner stared straight in front of him at the Malay arms, krises and parangs, which hung on the wall above the sofa on which his wife sat.

"It wasn't till I went back to Kuala Solor a year and a half later that I found out why their manner had seemed so odd." Millicent gave a queer little sound like the echo of a scornful laugh. "I knew then a good deal that I hadn't known before. Harold came to England that time in order to marry. He didn't much mind who it was. Do you remember how we spread ourselves out to catch him, mother? We needn't have taken so much trouble."

"I don't know what you mean, Millicent," said Mrs. Skinner, not without acerbity, for the insinuation of scheming did not please her. "I saw he was attracted by you."

Millicent shrugged her heavy shoulders.

"He was a confirmed drunkard. He used to go to bed every night with a bottle of whisky and empty it before morning. The Chief Secretary told him he'd have to resign unless he stopped drinking. He said he'd give him one more chance. He could take his leave then and go to England. He advised him to marry so that when he got back he'd have some one to look after him. Harold married me because he wanted a keeper. They took bets in Kuala Solor on how long I'd make him stay sober."

"But he was in love with you," Mrs. Skinner interrupted. "You don't know how he used to speak to me about you, and at that time you're speaking of, when you went to Kuala Solor to have Joan, he wrote me such a charming letter about you."

Millicent looked at her mother again and a deep colour dyed her sallow skin. Her hands, lying on her lap, began to tremble a little. She thought of those first months of her married life. The Government launch took them to the mouth of the river and they spent the night at the bungalow which Harold said jokingly was their seaside residence. Next day they went up-stream in a prahu. From the novels she had read she expected the rivers of Borneo to be dark and strangely sinister, but the sky was blue, dappled with little white clouds, and the green of the mangroves and the nipas, washed by the flowing water, glistened in the sun. On each side stretched the pathless jungle, and in the distance, silhouetted against the sky, was the rugged outline of a mountain. The air in the early morning was fresh and buoyant. She seemed to enter upon a friendly, fertile land, and she had a sense of spacious freedom. They watched the banks for monkeys sitting on the branches of the tangled trees and once Harold pointed out something that looked like a log and said it was a crocodile. The Assistant Resident, in ducks and a topee, was at the landing-stage to meet them, and a dozen trim little soldiers were lined up to do them honour. The Assistant Resident was introduced to her. His name was Simpson.

"By Jove, sir," he said to Harold, "I'm glad to see you back. It's been deuced lonely without you."

The Resident's bungalow, surrounded by a garden in which grew wildly all manner of gay flowers, stood on the top of a low hill. It was a trifle shabby and the furniture was sparse, but the rooms were cool and of generous size.

"The kampong is down there," said Harold, pointing.

Her eyes followed his gesture, and from among the coconut trees rose the beating of a gong. It gave her a queer little sensation in the heart.

Though she had nothing much to do the days passed easily enough. At dawn a boy brought them their tea and they lounged about the verandah, enjoying the fragrance of the morning (Harold in a singlet and a sarong, she in a dressing-gown), till it was time to dress for breakfast. Then Harold went to his office and she spent an hour or two learning Malay. After tiffin he went back to his office while she slept. A cup of tea revived them both and they went for a walk or played golf on the nine hole links which Harold had made on a level piece of cleared jungle below the bungalow. Night fell at six and Mr. Simpson came along to have a drink. They chatted till their late dinner hour, and sometimes Harold and Mr. Simpson played chess. The balmy evenings were enchanting. The fireflies turned the bushes just below the verandah into coldly sparkling, tremulous beacons, and flowering trees scented the air with sweet odours. After dinner they read the papers which had left London six weeks before and presently went to bed. Millicent enjoyed being a married woman, with a house of her own, and she was pleased with the native servants, in their gay sarongs, who went about the bungalow, with bare feet, silent but friendly. It gave her a

pleasant sense of importance to be the wife of the
Resident. Harold impressed her by the fluency with
which he spoke the language, by his air of command,
and by his dignity. She went into the court-house
now and then to hear him try cases. The multi-
fariousness of his duties and the competent way in
which he performed them aroused her respect. Mr.
Simpson told her that Harold understood the natives
as well as any man in the country. He had the com-
bination of firmness, tact and good humour which
was essential in dealing with that timid, revengeful
and suspicious race. Millicent began to feel a certain admiration for her husband.

They had been married nearly a year when two
English naturalists came to stay with them for a few
days on their way to the interior. They brought
a pressing recommendation from the Governor and
Harold said he wanted to do them proud. Their
arrival was an agreeable change. Millicent asked
Mr. Simpson to dinner (he lived at the Fort and
only dined with them on Sunday nights) and after
dinner the men sat down to play bridge. Millicent
left them presently and went to bed, but they were
so noisy that for some time she could not get to sleep.
She did not know at what hour she was awakened
by Harold staggering into the room. She kept
silent. He made up his mind to have a bath before
getting into bed; the bath-house was just below their
room and he went down the steps that led to it. Ap-
parently he slipped, for there was a great clatter,
and he began to swear. Then he was violently sick.
She heard him sluice the buckets of water over him-

self and in a little while, walking very cautiously this time, he crawled up the stairs and slipped into bed. Millicent pretended to be asleep. She was disgusted. Harold was drunk. She made up her mind to speak about it in the morning. What would the naturalists think of him? But in the morning Harold was so dignified that she hadn't quite the determination to refer to the matter. At eight Harold and she, with their two guests, sat down to breakfast. Harold looked round the table.

"Porridge," he said. "Millicent, your guests might manage a little Worcester Sauce for breakfast, but I don't think they'll much fancy anything else. Personally I shall content myself with a whisky and soda."

The naturalists laughed, but shamefacedly.

"Your husband's a terror," said one of them.

"I should not think I had properly performed the duties of hospitality if I sent you sober to bed on the first night of your visit," said Harold, with his round, stately way of putting things.

Millicent, smiling acidly, was relieved to think that her guests had been as drunk as her husband. The next evening she sat up with them and the party broke up at a reasonable hour. But she was glad when the strangers went on with their journey. Their life resumed its placid course. Some months later Harold went on a tour of inspection of his district and came back with a bad attack of malaria. This was the first time she had seen the disease of which she had heard so much, and when he recovered it did not seem strange to her that Harold was very shaky. She found his manner peculiar. He would come back from the office and stare at her with glazed eyes; he would stand on the verandah, swaying slightly, but still dignified, and make long harangues about the political situation in England; losing the thread of his discourse, he would look at her with an archness which his natural stateliness made somewhat disconcerting and say:

"Pulls you down dreadfully, this confounded malaria. Ah, little woman, you little know the strain it puts upon a man to be an empire builder."

She thought that Mr. Simpson began to look worried, and once or twice, when they were alone, he seemed on the point of saying something to her which his shyness at the last moment prevented. The feeling grew so strong that it made her nervous and one evening when Harold, she knew not why, had remained later than usual at the office she tackled him.

"What have you got to say to me, Mr. Simpson?" she broke out suddenly.

He blushed and hesitated.

"Nothing. What makes you think I have anything in particular to say to you?"

Mr. Simpson was a thin, weedy youth of four and twenty, with a fine head of waving hair which he took great pains to plaster down very flat. His wrists were swollen and scarred with mosquito bites. Millicent looked at him steadily.

"If it's something to do with Harold, don't you think it would be kinder to tell me frankly?"

He grew scarlet now. He shuffled uneasily on his rattan chair. She insisted.

"I'm afraid you'll think it awful cheek," he said at last. "It's rotten of me to say anything about my chief behind his back. Malaria's a rotten thing and after one's had a bout of it one feels awfully down and out."

He hesitated again. The corners of his mouth sagged as if he were going to cry. To Millicent he seemed like a little boy.

"I'll be as silent as the grave," she said with a smile, trying to conceal her apprehension. "Do tell me."

"I think it's a pity your husband keeps a bottle of whisky at the office. He's apt to take a nip more often than he otherwise would."

Mr. Simpson's voice was hoarse with agitation. Millicent felt a sudden coldness shiver through her. She controlled herself, for she knew that she must not frighten the boy if she were to get out of him all there was to tell. He was unwilling to speak. She pressed him, wheedling, appealing to his sense of duty, and at last she began to cry. Then he told her that Harold had been drunk more or less for the last fortnight, the natives were talking about it, and they said that soon he would be as bad as he had been before his marriage. He had been in the habit of drinking a good deal too much then, but details of that time, notwithstanding all her attempts, Mr. Simpson resolutely declined to give her.

"Do you think he's drinking now?" she asked.

"I don't know."

Millicent felt herself on a sudden hot with shame and anger. The Fort, as it was called because the rifles and the ammunition were kept there, was also the court-house. It stood opposite the Resident's bungalow in a garden of its own. The sun was just about to set and she did not need a hat. She got up and walked across. She found Harold sitting in the office behind the large hall in which he administered justice. There was a bottle of whisky in front of him. He was smoking cigarettes and talking to three or four Malays who stood in front of him listening with obsequious and at the same time scornful smiles. His face was red.

The natives vanished.

"I came to see what you were doing," she said.

He rose, for he always treated her with elaborate politeness, and lurched. Feeling himself unsteady he assumed an elaborate stateliness of demeanour.

"Take a seat, my dear, take a seat. I was detained by press of work."

She looked at him with angry eyes.

"You're drunk," she said.

He stared at her, his eyes bulging a little, and a haughty look gradually traversed his large and fleshy face.

"I haven't the remotest idea what you mean," he said.

She had been ready with a flow of wrathful expostulation, but suddenly she burst into tears. She sank into a chair and hid her face. Harold looked at her for an instant, then the tears began to trickle down his cheeks; he came towards her with outstretched arms and fell heavily on his knees. Sobbing, he clasped her to him.

"Forgive me, forgive me," he said. "I promise you it shall not happen again. It was that damned malaria."

"It's so humiliating," she moaned.

He wept like a child. There was something very touching in the self-abasement of that big dignified man. Presently Millicent looked up. His eyes, appealing and contrite, sought hers.

"Will you give me your word of honour that you'll never touch liquor again?"

"Yes, yes. I hate it."

It was then she told him that she was with child. He was overjoyed.

"That is the one thing I wanted. That'll keep me straight."

They went back to the bungalow. Harold bathed himself and had a nap. After dinner they talked long and quietly. He admitted that before he married her he had occasionally drunk more than was good for him: in outstations it was easy to fall into bad habits. He agreed to everything that Millicent asked. And during the months before it was necessary for her to go to Kuala Solor for her confinement Harold was an excellent husband, tender, thoughtful, proud and affectionate: he was irreproachable. A launch came to fetch her, she was to leave him for six weeks, and he promised faithfully to drink nothing during her absence. He put his hands on her shoulders.

"I never break a promise," he said in his dignified way. "But even without it, can you imagine that while you are going through so much, I should do anything to increase your troubles?"

Joan was born. Millicent stayed at the Resident's and Mrs. Gray, his wife, a kindly creature of middle age, was very good to her. The two women had little to do during the long hours they were alone but to talk, and in course of time Millicent learnt everything there was to know of her husband's alcoholic past. The fact which she found most difficult to reconcile herself to was that Harold had been told that the only condition upon which he would be allowed to keep his post was that he should bring back a wife. It caused in her a dull feeling of resentment. And when she discovered what a persistent drunkard he had been she felt vaguely uneasy. She had a horrid fear that during her absence he would not have been able to resist the craving. She went home with her baby and a nurse. She spent a night at the mouth of the river and sent a messenger in a canoe to announce her arrival. She scanned the landing-stage anxiously as the launch approached it. Harold and Mr. Simpson were standing there. The trim little soldiers were lined up. Her heart sank, for Harold was swaying slightly, like a man who seeks to keep his balance on a rolling ship, and she knew he was drunk.

It wasn't a very pleasant home-coming. She had almost forgotten her mother and father and her sister who sat there silently listening to her. Now she roused herself and became once more aware of their presence. All that she spoke of seemed very far away.

"I knew that I hated him then," she said. "I could have killed him."

"Oh, Millicent, don't say that," cried her mother. "Don't forget that he's dead, poor man."

Millicent looked at her mother, and for a moment a scowl darkened her impassive face. Mr. Skinner moved uneasily.

"Go on," said Kathleen.

"When he found out that I knew all about him he didn't bother very much more. In three months he had another attack of D. T.'s."

"Why didn't you leave him?" said Kathleen.

"What would have been the good of that? He would have been dismissed from the service in a fortnight. Who was to keep me and Joan? I had to stay. And when he was sober I had nothing to complain of. He wasn't in the least in love with me, but he was fond of me: I hadn't married him because I was in love with him but because I wanted to be married. I did everything I could to keep liquor from him; I managed to get Mr. Gray to prevent whisky being sent from Kuala Solor, but he got it from the Chinese. I watched him as a cat watches a mouse. He was too cunning for me. In a little while he had another outbreak. He neglected his duties. I was afraid complaints would be made. We were two days from Kuala Solor and that was our safeguard, but I suppose something was said, for Mr. Gray wrote a private letter of warning to me. I showed it to Harold. He stormed and blustered, but I saw he was frightened, and for two or three months he was quite sober. Then he began again. And so it went on till our leave became due.

"Before we came to stay here I begged and prayed him to be careful. I didn't want any of you to know what sort of a man I had married. All the time he was in England he was all right and before we sailed I warned him. He'd grown to be very fond of Joan, and very proud of her, and she was devoted to him. She always liked him better than she liked me. I asked him if he wanted to have his child grow up knowing that he was a drunkard, and I found out that at last I'd got a hold on him. The thought terrified him. I told him that *I* wouldn't allow it, and if he ever let Joan see him drunk I'd take her away from him at once. Do you know, he grew quite pale when I said it. I fell on my knees that night and thanked God because I'd found a way of saving my husband.

"He told me that if I would stand by him he would have another try. We made up our minds to fight the thing together. And he tried so hard. When he felt as though he *must* drink he came to me. You know he was inclined to be rather pompous: with me he was so humble, he was like a child; he depended on me. Perhaps he didn't love me when he married me, but he loved me then, me and Joan. I'd hated him, because of the humiliation, because when he was drunk and tried to be dignified and impressive he was loathsome; but now I got a strange feeling in my heart. It wasn't love, but it was a queer, shy tenderness. He was something more than my husband, he was like a child that I'd carried under my heart for long and weary months. He was so proud of me and you know, I was proud too. His long speeches didn't irritate me any more and I only thought his stately ways rather funny and charming. At last we won. For two years he never touched a drop. He lost his craving entirely. He was even able to joke about it.

"Mr. Simpson had left us then and we had another young man called Francis.

" 'I'm a reformed drunkard you know, Francis,' Harold said to him once. If it hadn't been for my wife I'd have been sacked long ago. I've got the best wife in the world, Francis.'

"You don't know what it meant to me to hear him say that. I felt that all I'd gone through was worth while. I was so happy."

She was silent. She thought of the broad, yellow and turbid river on whose banks she had lived so long. The egrets, white and gleaming in the tremulous sunset, flew down the stream in a flock, flew low and swift, and scattered. They were like a ripple of snowy notes, sweet and pure and spring-like, which an unseen hand drew forth, a divine arpeggio, from an unseen harp. They fluttered along between the green banks, wrapped in the shadows of evening, like the happy thoughts of a contented mind.

"Then Joan fell ill. For three weeks we were very anxious. There was no doctor nearer than Kuala Solor and we had to put up with the treatment of a native dispenser. When she grew well again I took her down to the mouth of the river in order to give her a breath of sea air. We stayed there a week. It was the first time I had been separated from Harold since I went away to have Joan. There was a fishing village, on piles, not far from us, but really we were quite alone. I thought a great deal about Harold, so tenderly, and all at once I knew that I loved him. I was so glad when the prahu came to fetch us back, because I wanted to tell him. I thought it would mean a good deal to him. I can't tell you how happy I was. As we rowed up-stream the headman told me that Mr. Francis had had to go up-country to arrest a woman who had murdered her husband. He had been gone a couple of days.

"I was surprised that Harold was not on the landing-stage to meet me; he was always very punctilious about that sort of thing; he used to say that husband and wife should treat one another as politely as they treated acquaintances; and I could not imagine what business had prevented him. I walked up the little hill on which the bungalow stood. The ayah brought Joan behind me. The bungalow was strangely silent. There seemed to be no servants about and I could not make it out; I wondered if Harold hadn't expected me so soon and was out. I went up the steps. Joan was thirsty and the ayah took her to the servants' quarters to give her something to drink. Harold was not in the sitting-room. I called him, but there was no answer. I was disappointed, because I should have liked him to be there. I went into our bedroom. Harold wasn't out after all: he was lying on the bed asleep. I was really very much amused because he always pretended he never slept in the afternoon. He said it was an unnecessary habit that we white people got into. I went up to the bed softly. I thought I would have a joke with him. I opened the mosquito curtains. He was lying on his back, with nothing on but a sarong, and there was an empty whisky bottle by his side. He was drunk.

"It had begun again. All my struggles for so many years were wasted. My dream was shattered. It was all hopeless. I was seized with rage."

Millicent's face grew once again darkly red and she clenched the arms of the chair she sat in.

"I took him by the shoulders and shook him with all my might. 'You beast,' I cried, 'you beast.' I was so angry I don't know what I did, I don't know what I said. I kept on shaking him. You don't know how loathsome he looked, that large fat man, half naked; he hadn't shaved for days, and his face was bloated and purple. He was breathing heavily. I shouted at him, but he took no notice. I tried to drag him out of bed, but he was too heavy. He lay there like a log. 'Open your eyes,' I screamed. I shook him again. I hated him. I hated him all the more because for a week I'd loved him with all my heart. He'd let me down. He'd let me down. I wanted to tell him what a filthy beast he was. I could make no impression on him. 'You shall open your eyes,' I cried. I was determined to make him look at me."

The widow licked her dry lips. Her breath seemed hurried. She was silent.

"If he was in that state I should have thought it best to have let him go on sleeping," said Kathleen.

"There was a parang on the wall by the side of the bed. You know how fond Harold was of curios."

"What's a parang?" said Mrs. Skinner.

"Don't be silly, mother," her husband replied irritably. "There's one on the wall immediately behind you."

He pointed to the Malay sword on which for some reason his eyes had been unconsciously resting. Mrs. Skinner drew quickly into the corner of the sofa, with a little frightened gesture, as though she had been told that a snake lay curled up beside her.

"Suddenly the blood spurted out from Harold's throat. There was a great red gash right across it."

"Millicent," cried Kathleen, springing up and almost leaping towards her, "what in God's name do you mean?"

Mrs. Skinner stood staring at her with wide startled eyes, her mouth open.

"The parang wasn't on the wall any more. It was on the bed. Then Harold opened his eyes. They were just like Joan's."

"I don't understand," said Mr. Skinner. "How could he have committed suicide if he was in the state you describe?"

Kathleen took her sister's arm and shook her angrily.

"Millicent, for God's sake, explain."

Millicent released herself.

"The parang was on the wall, I told you. I don't know what happened. There was all the blood and Harold opened his eyes. He died almost at once. He never spoke, but he gave a sort of gasp."

At last Mr. Skinner found his voice.

"But, you wretched woman, it was murder."

Millicent, her face mottled with red, gave him such a look of scornful hatred that he shrank back. Mrs. Skinner cried out.

"Millicent, you didn't do it, did you?"

Then Millicent did something that made them all feel as though their blood were turned to ice in their veins. She chuckled.

"I don't know who else did," she said.

"My God," muttered Mr. Skinner.

Kathleen had been standing bolt upright, with her hands to her heart, as though its beating were intolerable.

"And what happened then?" she said.

"I screamed. I went to the window and flung it open. I called for the ayah. She came across the compound with Joan. 'Not Joan,' I cried. 'Don't let her come.' She called the cook and told him to take the child. I cried to her to hurry. And when she came I showed her Harold. 'The Tuan's killed himself!' I cried. She gave a scream and ran out of the house.

"No one would come near. They were all frightened out of their wits. I wrote a letter to Mr. Francis, telling him what had happened, and asking him to come at once."

"How do you mean you told him what had happened?"

"I said, on my return from the mouth of the river, I'd found Harold with his throat cut. You know, in the tropics you have to bury people quickly. I got a Chinese coffin, and the soldiers dug a grave behind the Fort. When Mr. Francis came Harold had been buried for nearly two days. He was only a boy. I could do anything I wanted with him. I told him I'd found the parang in Harold's hand and there was no doubt he'd killed himself in an attack of *delirium tremens*. I showed him the empty bottle. The servants said he'd been drinking hard ever since I left to go to the sea. I told the same story at Kuala Solor. Every one was very kind to me, and the Government granted me a pension."

For a little while nobody spoke. At last Mr. Skinner gathered himself together.

"I am a member of the legal profession. I'm a solicitor. I have certain duties. We've always had a most respectable practice. You've put me in a monstrous position."

He fumbled, searching for the phrases that played at hide and seek in his scattered wits. Millicent looked at him with scorn.

"What are you going to do about it?"

"It was murder, that's what it was; do you think I can possibly connive at it?"

"Don't talk nonsense, father," said Kathleen sharply. "You can't give your own daughter up."

"You've put me in a monstrous position," he repeated.

Millicent shrugged her shoulders again.

"You made me tell you. And I've borne it long enough by myself. It was time that all of you bore it too."

At that moment the door was opened by the maid.

"Davis has brought the car round, sir," she said.

Kathleen had the presence of mind to say something, and the maid withdrew.

"We'd better be starting," said Millicent.

"I can't go to the party now," cried Mrs. Skinner, with horror. "I'm far too upset. How can we face the Heywoods? And the Bishop will want to be introduced to you."

Millicent made a gesture of indifference. Her eyes held their ironical expression.

"We must go, mother," said Kathleen. "It would look so funny if we stayed away." She turned on Millicent furiously. "Oh, I think the whole thing is such frightfully bad form."

Mrs. Skinner looked helplessly at her husband. He went to her and gave her his hand to help her up from the sofa.

"I'm afraid we must go, mother," he said.

"And me with the ospreys in my toque that Harold gave me with his own hands," she moaned.

He led her out of the room, Kathleen followed close on their heels, and a step or two behind came Millicent.

"You'll get used to it, you know," she said quietly. "At first I thought of it all the time, but now I forget it for two or three days together. It's not as if there was any danger."

They did not answer. They walked through the hall and out of the front door. The three ladies got into the back of the car and Mr. Skinner seated himself beside the driver. They had no self-starter; it was an old car, and Davis went to the bonnet to crank it up. Mr. Skinner turned round and looked petulantly at Millicent.

"I ought never to have been told," he said. "I think it was most selfish of you."

Davis took his seat and they drove off to the Canon's garden-party.

P. & O.

P. & O.

MRS. HAMLYN lay on her long chair and lazily watched the passengers come along the gangway. The ship had reached Singapore in the night and since dawn had been taking on cargo; the winches had been grinding away all day, but by now her ears were accustomed to their insistent clamour. She had lunched at the Europe and for lack of anything better to do had driven in a rickshaw through the gay, multitudinous streets of the city. Singapore is the meeting-place of many races. The Malays, though natives of the soil, dwell uneasily in towns, and are few; and it is the Chinese, supple, alert and industrious, who throng the streets, the dark-skinned Tamils walk on their silent, naked feet as though they were but brief sojourners in a strange land, but the Bengalis, sleek and prosperous, are easy in their surroundings and self-assured; the sly and obsequious Japanese seem busy with pressing and secret affairs; and the English in their topees and white ducks, speeding past in motor-cars or at leisure in their rickshaws, wear a nonchalant and careless air. The rulers of these teeming peoples take their authority with a smiling unconcern. And now, tired and hot, Mrs. Hamlyn waited for the ship to set out again on her long journey across the Indian Ocean.

She waved a rather large hand, for she was a big woman, to the doctor and Mrs. Linsell as they came on board. She had been on the ship since she left Yokohama, and had watched with acid amusement the intimacy which had sprung up between the two. Linsell was a naval officer who had been attached to the British Embassy at Tokio, and she had wondered at the indifference with which he took the attentions that the doctor paid his wife. Two men came along the gangway, new passengers, and she amused herself by trying to discover from their demeanour whether they were married or single. Close by, a group of men were sitting together on rattan chairs, planters she judged by their khaki suits and wide-brimmed double felt hats, and they kept the deck-steward busy with their orders. They were talking loudly and laughing, for they had all drunk enough to make them somewhat foolishly hilarious, and they were evidently giving one of their number a send-off; but Mrs. Hamlyn could not tell which it was that was to be a fellow-passenger. The time was growing short. More passengers arrived, and then Mr. Jephson with dignity strolled up the gangway. He was a consul and was going home on leave. He had joined the ship at Shanghai and had immediately set about making himself agreeable to Mrs. Hamlyn. But just then she was disinclined for anything in the nature of a flirtation. She frowned as she thought of the reason which was taking her back to England. She would be spending Christmas at sea, far from any one who cared two straws for her, and for a moment she felt a little twist at her heartstrings; it vexed her that a subject which she was so resolute to put away from her should so constantly intrude on her unwilling mind.

But a warning bell clanged loudly and there was a general movement among the men who sat beside her.

"Well, if we don't want to be taken on we'd better be toddling," said one of them.

They rose and walked towards the gangway. Now that they were all shaking hands she saw who it was that they had come to see the last of. There was nothing very interesting about the man on whom Mrs. Hamlyn's eyes rested, but because she had nothing better to do she gave him more than a casual glance. He was a big fellow, well over six feet high, broad and stout; he was dressed in a bedraggled suit of khaki drill and his hat was battered and shabby. His friends left him, but they bandied chaff from the quay, and Mrs. Hamlyn noticed that he had a strong Irish brogue; his voice was full, loud and hearty.

Mrs. Linsell had gone below and the doctor came and sat down beside Mrs. Hamlyn. They told one another their small adventures of the day. The bell sounded again and presently the ship slid away from the wharf. The Irishman waved a last farewell to his friends and then sauntered towards the chair on which he had left papers and magazines. He nodded to the doctor.

"Is that some one you know?" asked Mrs. Hamlyn.

"I was introduced to him at the club before tiffin. His name is Gallagher. He's a planter."

After the hubbub of the port and the noisy bustle of departure, the silence of the ship was marked and grateful. They steamed slowly past green-clad, rocky cliffs (the P. & O. anchorage was in a charming and secluded cove), and came out into the main harbour. Ships of all nations lay at anchor, a great multitude, passenger boats, tugs, lighters, tramps; and beyond, behind the breakwater, you saw the crowded masts, a bare straight forest, of the native junks. In the soft light of the evening the busy scene was strangely touched with mystery, and you felt that all those vessels, their activity for the moment suspended, waited for some event of a peculiar significance.

Mrs. Hamlyn was a bad sleeper and when the dawn broke she was in the habit of going on deck. It rested her troubled heart to watch the last faint stars fade before the encroaching day and at that early hour the glassy sea had often an immobility which seemed to make all earthly sorrows of little consequence. The light was wan, and there was a pleasant shiver in the air. But next morning when she went to the end of the promenade deck, she found that some one was up before her. It was Gallagher. He was watching the low coast of Sumatra which the sunrise like a magician seemed to call forth from the dark sea. She was startled and a little vexed, but before she could turn away he had seen her and nodded.

"Up early," he said. "Have a cigarette?"

He was in pyjamas and slippers. He took his case from his coat pocket and handed it to her. She hesitated. She had on nothing but a dressing-gown and a little lace cap which she had put over her tousled hair, and she knew that she must look a sight; but she had her reasons for scourging her soul.

"I suppose a woman of forty has no right to mind how she looks," she smiled, as though he must know what vain thoughts occupied her. She took the cigarette. "But you're up early too."

"I'm a planter. I've had to get up at five in the morning for so many years that I don't know how I'm going to get out of the habit."

"You'll not find it will make you very popular at home."

She saw his face better now that it was not shadowed by a hat. It was agreeable without being handsome. He was of course much too fat, and his features which must have been good enough when he was a young man were thickened. His skin was red and bloated. But his dark eyes were merry; and though he could not have been less than five and forty his hair was black and thick. He gave you an impression of great strength. He was a heavy, ungraceful, commonplace man, and Mrs. Hamlyn, except for the promiscuity of shipboard, would never have thought it worth while to talk to him.

"Are you going home on leave?" she hazarded.

"No, I'm going home for good."

His black eyes twinkled. He was of a communicative turn, and before it was time for Mrs. Hamlyn to go below in order to have her bath he had told

her a good deal about himself. He had been in the
Federated Malay States for twenty-five years, and
for the last ten had managed an estate in Selantan.
It was a hundred miles from anything that could be
described as civilisation and the life had been lonely;
but he had made money; during the rubber boom he
had done very well and with an astuteness which
was unexpected in a man who looked so happy-go-
lucky he had invested his savings in Government
stock. Now that the slump had come he was prepared to retire.

"What part of Ireland do you come from?" asked
Mrs. Hamlyn.

"Galway."

Mrs. Hamlyn had once motored through Ireland
and she had a vague recollection of a sad and moody
town with great stone warehouses, deserted and
crumbling, which faced the melancholy sea. She had
a sensation of greenness and of soft rain, of silence
and of resignation. Was it here that Mr. Gallagher
meant to spend the rest of his life? He spoke of it
with boyish eagerness. The thought of his vitality
in that grey world of shadows was so incongruous
that Mrs. Hamlyn was intrigued.

"Does your family live there?" she asked.

"I've got no family. My mother and father are
dead. So far as I know I haven't a relation in the
world."

He had made all his plans, he had been making
them for twenty-five years, and he was pleased to
have some one to talk to of all these things that he
had been obliged for so long only to talk to himself

about. He meant to buy a house and he would keep a motor-car. He was going to breed horses. He didn't much care about shooting; he had shot a lot of big game during his first years in the F.M.S.; but now he had lost his zest. He didn't see why the beasts of the jungle should be killed; he had lived in the jungle so long. But he could hunt.

"Do you think I'm too heavy?" he asked.

Mrs. Hamlyn, smiling, looked him up and down with appraising eyes.

"You must weigh a ton," she said.

He laughed. The Irish horses were the best in the world, and he'd always kept pretty fit. You had a devil of a lot of walking exercise on a rubber estate and he'd played a good deal of tennis. He'd soon get thin in Ireland. Then he'd marry. Mrs. Hamlyn looked silently at the sea, coloured now with the tenderness of the sunrise. She sighed.

"Was it easy to drag up all your roots? Is there no one you regret leaving behind? I should have thought after so many years, however much you'd looked forward to going home, when the time came at last to go it must have given you a pang."

"I was glad to get out. I was fed up. I never want to see the country again or any one in it."

One or two early passengers now began to walk round the deck and Mrs. Hamlyn, remembering that she was scantily clad, went below.

During the next day or two she saw little of Mr. Gallagher who passed his time in the smoking-room. Owing to a strike the ship was not touching at Colombo and the passengers settled down to a pleasant voyage across the Indian Ocean. They played deck games, they gossiped about one another, they flirted. The approach of Christmas gave them an occupation, for some one had suggested that there should be a fancy-dress dance on Christmas day, and the ladies set about making their dresses. A meeting was held of the first-class passengers to decide whether the second-class passengers should be invited, and notwithstanding the heat the discussion was animated. The ladies said that the second-class passengers would only feel ill-at-ease. On Christmas day it was to be expected that they would drink more than was good for them and unpleasantness might ensue. Every one who spoke insisted that there was in his (or her) mind no idea of class distinction, no one would be so snobbish as to think there was any difference between first- and second-class passengers as far as that went, but it would really be kinder to the second-class passengers not to put them in a false position. They would enjoy themselves much more if they had a party of their own in the second-class cabin. On the other hand, no one wanted to hurt their feelings, and of course one had to be more democratic nowadays (this was in reply to the wife of a missionary in China who said she had travelled on the P. & O. for thirty-five years and she had never heard of the second-class passengers being invited to a dance in the first-class saloon) and even though they wouldn't enjoy it, they might like to come. Mr. Gallagher, dragged unwillingly from the card-table, because it had been foreseen that the voting would be close, was asked his opinion by the consul.   He was taking home in the second-class a man who had been employed on his estate.   He raised his massive bulk from the couch on which he sat.

"As far as I'm concerned I've only got this to say: I've got the man who was looking after our engines with me.   He's a rattling good fellow and he's just as fit to come to your party as I am.   But he won't come because I'm going to make him so drunk on Christmas day that by six o'clock he'll be fit for nothing but to be put to bed."

Mr. Jephson, the consul, gave a distorted smile. On account of his official position he had been chosen to preside at the meeting and he wished the matter to be taken seriously.   He was a man who often said that if a thing was worth doing it was worth doing well.

"I gather from your observations," he said, not without acidity, "that the question before the meeting does not seem to you of great importance."

"I don't think it matters a tinker's curse," said Gallagher, with twinkling eyes.

Mrs. Hamlyn laughed.   The scheme was at last devised to invite the second-class passengers, but to go to the captain privily and point out to him the advisability of withholding his consent to their coming into the first-class saloon.   It was on the evening of the day on which this happened that Mrs. Hamlyn, having dressed for dinner, came on deck at the same time as Mr. Gallagher.

"Just in time for a cocktail, Mrs. Hamlyn," he said jovially.

"I'd like one. To tell you the truth I need cheering up."

"Why?" he smiled.

Mrs. Hamlyn thought his smile attractive, but she did not want to answer his question.

"I told you the other morning," she answered cheerfully. "I'm forty."

"I never met a woman who insisted on the fact so much."

They went into the lounge and the Irishman ordered a dry Martini for her and a gin pahit for himself. He had lived too long in the East to drink anything else.

"You've got hiccups," said Mrs. Hamlyn.

"Yes, I've had them all the afternoon," he answered carelessly. "It's rather funny, they came on just as we got out of sight of land."

"I daresay they'll pass off after dinner."

They drank, the second bell rang, and they went into the dining-saloon.

"You don't play bridge?" he said, as they parted.

"No."

Mrs. Hamlyn did not notice that she saw nothing of Gallagher for two or three days. She was occupied with her own thoughts. They crowded upon her when she was sewing; they came between her and the novel with which she sought to cheat their insistence. She had hoped that as the ship took her further away from the scene of her unhappiness the torment of her mind would be eased; but contrariwise, each day that brought her nearer England increased her distress. She looked forward with dismay to the bleak emptiness of the life that awaited her; and then, turning her exhausted wits from a prospect that made her flinch, she considered, as she had done she knew not how many times before, the situation from which she had fled.

She had been married for twenty years. It was a long time and of course she could not expect her husband to be still madly in love with her; she was not madly in love with him; but they were good friends and they understood one another. Their marriage, as marriages go, might very well have been looked upon as a success. Suddenly she discovered that he had fallen in love. She would not have objected to a flirtation, he had had those before, and she had chaffed him about them; he had not minded that, it somewhat flattered him, and they had laughed together at an inclination which was neither deep nor serious. But this was different. He was in love as passionately as a boy of eighteen. He was fifty-two. It was ridiculous. It was indecent. And he loved without sense or prudence: by the time the hideous fact was forced upon her all the foreigners in Yokohama knew it. After the first shock of astonished anger, for he was the last man from whom such a folly might have been expected, she tried to persuade herself that she could have understood, and so have forgiven, if he had fallen in love with a girl. Middle-aged men often make fools of themselves with flappers, and after twenty years in the Far East she knew that the fifties were the dangerous age for men. But he had no excuse. He was in love with a woman eight years older than herself. It was grotesque, and

it made her, his wife, perfectly absurd. Dorothy
Lacom was hard on fifty. He had known her for
eighteen years, for Lacom, like her own husband,
was a silk merchant in Yokohama. Year in, year
out, they had seen one another three or four times
a week, and once, when they happened to be in England together, had shared a house at the seaside.
But nothing! Not till a year ago had there been
anything between them but a chaffing friendship. It
was incredible. Of course Dorothy was a handsome
woman; she had a good figure, overdeveloped, perhaps, but still comely; with bold black eyes and a
red mouth and lovely hair; but all that she had had
years before. She was forty-eight. Forty-eight!

Mrs. Hamlyn tackled her husband at once. At
first he swore that there was not a word of truth in
what she accused him of, but she had her proofs; he
grew sulky; and at last he admitted what he could
no longer deny. Then he said an astonishing thing.

"Why should you care?" he asked.

It maddened her. She answered him with angry
scorn. She was voluble, finding in the bitterness of
her heart wounding things to say. He listened to
her quietly.

"I've not been such a bad husband to you for the
twenty years we've been married. For a long time
now we've only been friends. I have a great affection for you and this hasn't altered it in the very
smallest degree. I'm giving Dorothy nothing that
I take away from you."

"But what have you to complain of in me?"

"Nothing. No man could want a better wife."

"How can you say that when you have the heart to treat me so cruelly?"

"I don't want to be cruel to you. I can't help myself."

"But what on earth made you fall in love with her?"

"How can I tell? You don't think I wanted to, do you?"

"Couldn't you have resisted?"

"I tried. I think we both tried."

"You talk as though you were twenty. Why, you're both middle-aged people. She's eight years older than I am. It makes me look such a perfect fool."

He did not answer. She did not know what emotions seethed in her heart. Was it jealousy that seemed to clutch at her throat, anger, or was it merely wounded pride?

"I'm not going to let it go on. If only you and she were concerned I would divorce you, but there's her husband and then there are the children. Good heavens, does it occur to you that if they were girls instead of boys she might be a grandmother by now?"

"Easily."

"What a mercy that we have no children!"

He put out an affectionate hand as though to caress her, but she drew back with horror.

"You've made me the laughing-stock of all my friends. For all our sakes I'm willing to hold my tongue, but only on the condition that everything stops now, at once, and for ever."

He looked down and played reflectively with a Japanese knick-knack that was on the table.

"I'll tell Dorothy what you say," he replied at last.

She gave him a little bow, silently, and walked past him out of the room. She was too angry to observe that she was somewhat melodramatic.

She waited for him to tell her the result of his interview with Dorothy Lacom, but he made no further reference to the scene. He was quiet, polite, and silent; and at last she was obliged to ask him.

"Have you forgotten what I said to you the other day?" she enquired frigidly.

"No. I talked to Dorothy. She wishes me to tell you that she is desperately sorry that she has caused you so much pain. She would like to come and see you, but she is afraid you wouldn't like it."

"What decision have you come to?"

He hesitated. He was very grave, but his voice trembled a little.

"I'm afraid there's no use in our making a promise we shouldn't be able to keep."

"That settles it then," she answered.

"I think I should tell you that if you brought an action for divorce we should have to contest it. You would find it impossible to get the necessary evidence and you would lose your case."

"I wasn't thinking of doing that. I shall go back to England and consult a lawyer. Nowadays these things can be managed fairly easily and I shall throw myself on your generosity. I daresay you will enable me to get my freedom without bringing Dorothy Lacom into the matter."

He sighed.

"It's an awful muddle, isn't it? I don't want you to divorce me, but of course I'll do anything I can to meet your wishes."

"What on earth do you expect me to do?" she cried, her anger rising again. "Do you expect me to sit still and be made a damned fool of?"

"I'm awfully sorry to put you in a humiliating position." He looked at her with harassed eyes. "I'm quite sure we didn't want to fall in love with one another. We're both of us very conscious of our age. Dorothy, as you say, is old enough to be a grandmother and I'm a baldish, stoutish gentleman of fifty-two. When you fall in love at twenty you think your love will last for ever, but at fifty you know so much, about life and about love, and you know that it will last so short a time." His voice was low and rueful. It was as though before his mind's eye he saw the sadness of autumn and the leaves falling from the trees. He looked at her gravely. "And at that age you feel that you can't afford to throw away the chance of happiness which a freakish destiny has given you. In five years it will certainly be over, and perhaps in six months. Life is rather drab and grey, and happiness is so rare. We shall be dead so long."

It gave Mrs. Hamlyn a bitter sensation of pain to hear her husband, a matter-of-fact and practical man, speak in a strain which was quite new to her. He had gained on a sudden a wistful and tragic personality of which she knew nothing. The twenty years during which they had lived together had no power over him and she was helpless in face of his determination. She could do nothing but go, and now, resentfully determined to get the divorce with which she had threatened him, she was on her way to England.

The smooth sea, upon which the sun beat down so that it shone like a sheet of glass, was as empty and hostile as life in which there was no place for her. For three days no other craft had broken in upon the solitariness of that expanse. Now and again its even surface was scattered for the twinkling of an eye by the scurry of flying fish. The heat was so great that even the most energetic of passengers had given up deck games and now (it was after luncheon) such as were not resting in their cabins lay about on chairs. Linsell strolled towards her and sat down.

"Where's Mrs. Linsell?" asked Mrs. Hamlyn.

"Oh, I don't know. She's about somewhere."

His indifference exasperated her. Was it possible that he did not see that his wife and the surgeon were falling in love with one another? Yet, not so very long ago, he must have cared. Their marriage had been romantic. They had become engaged when Mrs. Linsell was still at school and he little more than a boy. They must have been a charming, handsome pair, and their youth and their mutual love must have been touching. And now, after so short a time, they were tired of one another. It was heartbreaking. What had her husband said?

"I suppose you're going to live in London when

you get home?" asked Linsell lazily, for something to say.

"I suppose so," said Mrs. Hamlyn.

It was hard to reconcile herself to the fact that she had nowhere to go and where she lived mattered not in the least to any one alive. Some association of ideas made her think of Gallagher. She envied the eagerness with which he was returning to his native land, and she was touched, and at the same time amused, when she remembered the exuberant imagination he showed in describing the house he meant to live in and the wife he meant to marry. Her friends in Yokohama, apprised in confidence of her determination to divorce her husband, had assured her that she would marry again. She did not much want to enter a second time upon a state which had once so disappointed her, and besides, most men would think twice before they suggested marriage to a woman of forty. Mr. Gallagher wanted a buxom young person.

"Where is Mr. Gallagher?" she asked the submissive Linsell. "I haven't seen him for the last day or two."

"Didn't you know? He's ill."

"Poor thing. What's the matter with him?"

"He's got hiccups."

Mrs. Hamlyn laughed.

"Hiccups don't make one ill, do they?"

"The surgeon is rather worried. He's tried all sorts of things, but he can't stop them."

"How very odd."

She thought no more about it, but next morning, chancing upon the surgeon, she asked him how Mr. Gallagher was. She was surprised to see his boyish, cheerful face darken and grow perplexed.

"I'm afraid he's very bad, poor chap."

"With hiccups?" she cried in amazement.

It was a disorder that really it was impossible to take seriously.

"You see, he can't keep any food down. He can't sleep. He's fearfully exhausted. I've tried everything I can think of." He hesitated. "Unless I can stop them soon—I don't quite know what'll happen."

Mrs. Hamlyn was startled.

"But he's so strong. He seemed so full of vitality."

"I wish you could see him now."

"Would he like me to go and see him?"

"Come along."

Gallagher had been moved from his cabin into the ship's hospital, and as they approached it they heard a loud hiccup. The sound, perhaps owing to its connection with insobriety, had in it something ludicrous. But Gallagher's appearance gave Mrs. Hamlyn a shock. He had lost flesh and the skin hung about his neck in loose folds; under the sunburn his face was pale. His eyes, before, full of fun and laughter, were haggard and tormented. His great body was shaken incessantly by the hiccups, and now there was nothing ludicrous in the sound; to Mrs. Hamlyn, for no reason that she knew, it seemed strangely terrifying. He smiled when she came in.

"I'm sorry to see you like this," she said.

"I shan't die of it, you know," he gasped. "I shall reach the green shores of Erin all right."

There was a man sitting beside him and he rose as they entered.

"This is Mr. Pryce," said the surgeon. "He was in charge of the machinery on Mr. Gallagher's estate."

Mrs. Hamlyn nodded. This was the second-class passenger to whom Gallagher had referred when they had discussed the party which was to be given on Christmas day. He was a very small man, but sturdy, with a pleasantly impudent countenance and an air of self-assurance.

"Are you glad to be going home?" asked Mrs. Hamlyn.

"You bet I am, lady," he answered.

The intonation of the few words told Mrs. Hamlyn that he was a cockney and, recognising the cheerful, sensible, good-humoured and careless type, her heart warmed to him.

"You're not Irish?" she smiled.

"Not me, miss. London's my 'ome and I shan't be sorry to see it again, I can tell you."

Mrs. Hamlyn never thought it offensive to be called miss.

"Well, sir, I'll be getting along," he said to Gallagher, with the beginning of a gesture as though he were going to touch a cap which he hadn't got on.

Mrs. Hamlyn asked the sick man whether she could do anything for him and in a minute or two left him with the doctor. The little cockney was waiting outside the door.

"Can I speak to you a minute or two, miss?" he asked.

"Of course."

The hospital cabin was aft and they stood, leaning against the rail, and looked down on the well-deck where lascars and stewards off duty were lounging about on the covered hatches.

"I don't know exactly 'ow to begin," said Pryce, uncertainly, a serious look strangely changing his lively, puckered face. "I've been with Mr. Gallagher for four years now and a better gentleman you wouldn't find in a week of Sundays."

He hesitated again.

"I don't like it and that's the truth."

"What don't you like?"

"Well, if you ask me 'e's for it, and the doctor don't know it. I told 'im, but 'e won't listen to a word I say."

"You mustn't be too depressed, Mr. Pryce. Of course the doctor's young, but I think he's quite clever, and people don't die of hiccups, you know. I'm sure Mr. Gallagher will be all right in a day or two."

"You know when it come on? Just as we was out of sight of land. She said 'e'd never see 'is 'ome."

Mrs. Hamlyn turned and faced him. She stood a good three inches taller than he.

"What do you mean?"

"My belief is, it's a spell been put on 'im, if you understand what I mean. Medicine's going to do 'im no good. You don't know them Malay women like what I do."

For a moment Mrs. Hamlyn was startled, and because she was startled she shrugged her shoulders and laughed.

"Oh, Mr. Pryce, that's nonsense."

"That's what the doctor said when I told 'im. But you mark my words, 'e'll die before we see land again."

The man was so serious that Mrs. Hamlyn, vaguely uneasy, was against her will impressed.

"Why should any one cast a spell on Mr. Gallagher?" she asked.

'Well, it's a bit awkward speakin' of it to a lady."

"Please tell me."

Pryce was so embarrassed that at another time Mrs. Hamlyn would have had difficulty in concealing her amusement.

"Mr. Gallagher's lived a long time up-country, if you understand what I mean, and of course it's lonely, and you know what men are, miss."

"I've been married for twenty years," she replied, smiling.

"I beg your pardon, ma'am. The fact is he had a Malay girl living with him. I don't know 'ow long, ten or twelve years, I think. Well, when he made up 'is mind to come 'ome for good she didn't say nothing. She just sat there. He thought she'd carry on no end, but she didn't. Of course 'e provided for 'er all right, 'e gave 'er a little 'ouse for herself, an' 'e fixed it up so as so much should be paid 'er every month; 'e wasn't mean, I will say that for 'im, an' she knew all along as 'e'd be going some time. She didn't cry or anything. When 'e packed up all 'is things and sent them off she just sat there an' watched 'em go. And when 'e sold 'is furniture to the Chinks she never said a word. He'd give 'er all she wanted. And when it was time for 'im to go so as to catch the boat she just kep' on sitting, on the steps of the bungalow, you know, and she just looked an' said nothing. He wanted to say good-bye to 'er, same as any one would, an', would you believe it? she never even moved. 'Aren't you going to say good-bye to me?' he says. A rare funny look came over 'er face. And do you know what she says? 'You go,' she says; they 'ave a funny way of talking, them natives, not like we 'ave, 'you go,' she says, 'but I tell you that you will never come to your own country. When the land sinks into the sea death will come upon you, an' before them as goes with you sees the land again, death will have took you.' It gave me quite a turn."

"What did Mr. Gallagher say?" asked Mrs. Hamlyn.

"Oh, well, you know what 'e is. He just laughed. 'Always merry an' bright,' he says and he jumps into the motor, an' off we go."

Mrs. Hamlyn saw the bright and sunny road that ran through the rubber estates, with their trim green trees, carefully spaced, and their silence, and then wound its way up hill and down through the tangled jungle. The car raced on, driven by a reckless Malay, with its white passengers, past Malay houses that stood away from the road among the coconut trees, sequestered and taciturn, and through busy villages where the market-place was crowded with dark-

skinned little people in gay sarongs. Then towards
evening it reached the trim, modern town, with its
clubs and its golf links, its well-ordered rest-house, its
white people, and its railway station, from which the
two men could take the train to Singapore. And the
woman sat on the steps of the bungalow, empty till
the new manager moved in, and watched the road
down which the car had panted, watched the car as
it sped on, and watched till at last it was lost in
the shadow of the night.

"What was she like?" Mrs. Hamlyn asked.

"Oh, well, to my way of thinking them Malay
women are all very much alike, you know," Pryce
answered. "Of course she wasn't so young any more
and you know what they are, them natives, they
run to fat something terrible."

"Fat?"

The thought, absurdly enough, filled Mrs. Hamlyn with dismay.

"Mr. Gallagher was always one to do himself
well, if you understand what I mean."

The idea of corpulence at once brought Mrs.
Hamlyn back to common sense. She was impatient
with herself because for an instant she had seemed
to accept the little cockney's suggestion.

"It's perfectly absurd, Mr. Pryce. Fat women
can't throw spells on people at a distance of a thousand miles. In fact life is very difficult for a fat
woman any way."

"You can laugh, miss, but unless something's done,
you mark my words, the governor's for it. And

medicine ain't goin' to save him, not white man's medicine."

"Pull yourself together, Mr. Pryce. This fat lady had no particular grievance against Mr. Gallagher. As these things are done in the East he seems to have treated her very well. Why should she wish him any harm?"

"We don't know 'ow they look at things. Why, a man can live there for twenty years with one of them natives, and d'you think 'e knows what's goin' on in that black heart of hers? Not 'im!"

She could not smile at his melodramatic language, for his intensity was impressive. And she knew, if any one did, that the hearts of men, whether their skins are yellow or white or brown, are incalculable.

"But even if she felt angry with him, even if she hated him and wanted to kill him, what could she do?" It was strange that Mrs. Hamlyn with her questions was trying now, unconsciously, to reassure herself. "There's no poison that could start working after six or seven days."

"I never said it was poison."

"I'm sorry, Mr. Pryce," she smiled, "but I'm not going to believe in a magic spell, you know."

"You've lived in the East."

"Off and on for twenty years."

"Well, if you can say what they can do and what they can't, it's more than I can." He clenched his fist and beat it on the rail with sudden, angry violence. "I'm fed up with the bloody country. It's got on my nerves, that's what it is. We're no match for them, us white men, and that's a fact. If you'll excuse me I think I'll go an' 'ave a tiddley. I've got the jumps."

He nodded abruptly and left her. Mrs. Hamlyn watched him, a sturdy, shuffling little man in shabby khaki, slither down the companion into the waist of the ship, walk across it with bent head, and disappear into the second-class saloon. She did not know why he left with her a vague uneasiness. She could not get out of her mind that picture of a stout woman, no longer young, in a sarong, a coloured jacket and gold ornaments, who sat on the steps of a bungalow looking at an empty road. Her heavy face was painted, but in her large, tearless eyes there was no expression. The men who drove in the car were like schoolboys going home for the holidays. Gallagher gave a sigh of relief. In the early morning, under the bright sky, his spirits bubbled. The future was like a sunny road that wandered through a wide-flung, wooded plain.

Later in the day Mrs. Hamlyn asked the doctor how his patient did. The doctor shook his head.

"I'm done. I'm at the end of my tether." He frowned unhappily. "It's rotten luck, striking a case like this. It would be bad enough at home, but on board ship . . ."

He was an Edinburgh man, but recently qualified, and he was taking this voyage as a holiday before settling down to practice. He felt himself aggrieved. He wanted to have a good time and, faced with this mysterious illness, he was worried to death. Of course he was inexperienced, but he was doing every-

thing that could be done and it exasperated him to
suspect that the passengers thought him an ignorant
fool.

"Have you heard what Mr. Pryce thinks?" asked
Mrs. Hamlyn.

"I never heard such rot. I told the captain and
he's right up in the air. He doesn't want it talked
about. He thinks it'll upset the passengers."

"I'll be as silent as the grave."

The surgeon looked at her sharply.

"Of course you don't believe that there can be any
truth in nonsense of that sort?" he asked.

"Of course not." She looked out at the sea which
shone, blue and oily and still, all round them. "I've
lived in the East a long time," she added. "Strange
things happen there."

"This is getting on my nerves," said the doctor.

Near them two little Japanese gentlemen were
playing deck quoits. They were trim and neat in
their tennis shirts, white trousers and buckram
shoes. They looked very European, they even called
the score to one another in English, and yet somehow to look at them filled Mrs. Hamlyn at that
moment with a vague disquiet. Because they seemed
to wear so easily a disguise there was about them
something sinister. Her nerves too were on edge.

And presently, no one quite knew how, the notion
spread through the ship that Gallagher was be-
witched. While the ladies sat about on their deck-
chairs, stitching away at the costumes they were making for the fancy-dress party on Christmas day, they
gossiped about it in undertones, and the men in the

smoking-room talked of it over their cocktails. A good many of the passengers had lived long in the East and from the recesses of their memory they produced strange and inexplicable stories. Of course it was absurd to think seriously that Gallagher was suffering from a malignant spell, such things were impossible, and yet this and that was a fact and no one had been able to explain it. The doctor had to confess that he could suggest no cause for Gallagher's condition, he was able to give a physiological explanation, but why these terrible spasms should have suddenly assailed him he did not say. Feeling vaguely to blame, he tried to defend himself.

"Why, it's the sort of case you might never come across in the whole of your practice," he said. "It's rotten luck."

He was in wireless communication with passing ships and suggestions for treatment came from here and there.

"I've tried everything they tell me," he said irritably. "The doctor of the Japanese boat advised adrenalin. How the devil does he expect me to have adrenalin in the middle of the Indian Ocean?"

There was something impressive in the thought of this ship speeding through a deserted sea while to her from all parts came unseen messages. She seemed at that moment strangely alone and yet the centre of the world. In the lazaret the sick man, shaken by the cruel spasms, gasped for life. Then the passengers became conscious that the ship's course was altered and they heard that the captain had made up his mind to put in at Aden. Gallagher was to be landed there and taken to the hospital where he could have attention which on board was impossible. The chief engineer received orders to force his engines. The ship was an old one and she throbbed with the greater effort. The passengers had grown used to the sound and feel of her engines and now the greater vibration shook their nerves with a new sensation. It would not pass into each one's unconsciousness, but beat on their sensibilities so that each felt a personal concern. And still the wide sea was empty of traffic so that they seemed to traverse an empty world. And now the uneasiness which had descended upon the ship, but which no one had been willing to acknowledge, became a definite malaise. The passengers grew irritable, and people quarrelled over trifles which at another time would have seemed insignificant. Mr. Jephson made his hackneyed jokes, but no one any longer repaid him with a smile. The Linsells had an altercation and Mrs. Linsell was heard late at night walking round the deck with her husband, and uttering in a low, tense voice a stream of vehement reproaches. There was a violent scene in the smoking-room one night over a game of bridge, and the reconciliation which followed it was attended with general intoxication. People talked little of Gallagher, but he was seldom absent from their thoughts. They examined the route map. The doctor said now that Gallagher could not live more than three or four days and they discussed acrimoniously what was the shortest time in which Aden could be reached. What happened to him after he was landed was no affair of theirs; they did not want him to die on board.

Mrs. Hamlyn saw Gallagher every day. With the suddenness with which after tropical rain in the spring you seem to see the herbage grow before your very eyes, she saw him go to pieces. Already his skin hung loosely on his bones and his double chin was like the wrinkled wattle of a turkey-cock. His cheeks were sunken. You saw now how large his frame was and through the sheet under which he lay his bony structure was like the skeleton of a pre-historic giant. For the most part he lay with his eyes closed, torpid with morphia, but shaken still with terrible spasms and when now and again he opened his eyes they were preternaturally large; they looked at you vaguely, perplexed and troubled, from the depths of their bony sockets. But when, emerging from his stupor, he recognised Mrs. Hamlyn he forced a gallant smile to his lips.

"How are you, Mr. Gallagher?" she said.

"Getting along, getting along. I shall be all right when we get out of this confounded heat. Lord, how I look forward to a dip in the Atlantic. I'd give anything for a good long swim. I want to feel the cold grey sea of Galway beating against my chest."

Then the hiccup shook him from the crown of his head to the sole of his foot. Mr. Pryce and the stewardess shared the care of him. The little cockney's face wore no longer its look of impudent gaiety, but instead was sullen.

"The captain sent for me yesterday," he told Mrs.

Hamlyn when they were alone. "He gave me a rare talking to."

"What about?"

"He said 'e wouldn't 'ave all this hoodoo stuff. He said it was frightening the passengers and I'd better keep a watch on me tongue or I'd 'ave 'im to reckon with. It's not my doing. I never said a word except to you and the doctor."

"It's all over the ship."

"I know it is. D'you think it's only me that's saying it? All them lascars and the Chinese, they all know what's the matter with him. You don't think you can teach them much, do you? They know it ain't a natural illness."

Mrs. Hamlyn was silent. She knew through the amahs of some of the passengers that there was no one on the ship, except the whites, who doubted that the woman whom Gallagher had left in distant Selantan was killing him with her magic. All were convinced that as they sighted the barren rocks of Arabia his soul would be parted from his body.

"The captain says if he hears of me trying any hanky-panky he'll confine me to my cabin for the rest of the voyage," said Pryce suddenly, a surly frown on his puckered face.

"What do you mean by hanky-panky?"

He looked at her for a moment fiercely as though she too were an object of the anger he felt against the captain.

"The doctor's tried every damned thing he knows, and he's wirelessed all over the place, and what good

'as 'e done? Tell me that. Can't 'e see the man's
dying? There's only one way to save him now."

"What do you mean?"

"It's magic what's killing 'im, and it's only magic
what'll save him. Oh, don't you say it can't be done.
I've seen it with me own eyes." His voice rose, irritable and shrill. "I've seen a man dragged from
the jaws of death, as you might say, when they got
in a *pawang,* what we call a witch-doctor, an' 'e did
'is little tricks. I seen it with me own eyes, I tell
you."

Mrs. Hamlyn did not speak. Pryce gave her a
searching look.

"One of them lascars on board, he's a witch-doctor, same as the *pawang* thet we 'ave in the F.M.S.
An' 'e says he'll do it. Only he must 'ave a live animal. A cock would do."

"What do you want a live animal for?" Mrs.
Hamlyn asked, frowning a little.

The cockney looked at her with quick suspicion.

"If you take my advice you won't know anything
about it. But I tell you what, I'm going to leave no
stone unturned to save my governor. An' if the
captain 'ears of it and shuts me up in me cabin, well,
let 'im."

At that moment Mrs. Linsell came up and Pryce
with his quaint gesture of salute left them. Mrs.
Linsell wanted Mrs. Hamlyn to fit the dress she had
been making herself for the fancy-dress ball, and on
the way down to the cabin she spoke to her anxiously
about the possibility that Mr. Gallagher might die
on Christmas day. They could not possibly have

the dance if he did.   She had told the doctor that she
would never speak to him again if this happened, and
the doctor had promised her faithfully that he would
keep the man alive over Christmas day somehow.

"It would be nice for him, too," said Mrs. Linsell.

"For whom?" asked Mrs. Hamlyn.

"For poor Mr. Gallagher.   Naturally no one likes
to die on Christmas day.   Do they?"

"I don't really know," said Mrs. Hamlyn.

That night, after she had been asleep a little while,
she awoke weeping.   It dismayed her that she should
cry in her sleep.   It was as though then the weak-
ness of the flesh mastered her, and, her will broken,
she was defenceless against a natural sorrow.   She
turned over in her mind, as so often before, the
details of the disaster which had so profoundly affected her; she repeated the conversations with her
husband, wishing she had said this and blaming herself because she had said the other.   She wished with
all her heart that she had remained in comfortable
ignorance of her husband's infatuation, and asked
herself whether she would not have been wiser to
pocket her pride and shut her eyes to the unwelcome
truth.   She was a woman of the world and she knew
too well how much more she lost in separating herself from her husband than his love; she lost the settled establishment and the assured position, the
ample means and the support of a recognised back-
ground.   She had known of many separated wives,
living equivocally on smallish incomes, and knew
how quickly their friends found them tiresome.   And
she was lonely.   She was as lonely as the ship that

throbbed her hasting way through an unpeopled sea, and lonely as the friendless man who lay dying in the ship's lazaret. Mrs. Hamlyn knew that her thoughts had got the better of her now and that she would not easily sleep again. It was very hot in her cabin. She looked at the time; it was between four and half-past; she must pass two mortal hours before broke the reassuring day.

She slipped into a kimono and went on deck. The night was sombre and although the sky was un-clouded no stars were visible. Panting and shaking, the old ship under full steam lumbered through the darkness. The silence was uncanny. Mrs. Hamlyn with bare feet groped her way slowly along the de-serted deck. It was so black that she could see noth-ing. She came to the end of the promenade deck and leaned against the rail. Suddenly she started and her attention was fixed, for on the lower deck she caught a fitful glow. She leaned forward cautiously. It was a little fire, and she saw only the glow because the naked backs of men, crouched round, hid the flame. At the edge of the circle she divined, rather than saw, a stocky figure in pyjamas. The rest were natives, but this was a European. It must be Pryce and she guessed immediately that some dark cere-mony of exorcism was in progress. Straining her ears she heard a low voice muttering a string of se-cret words. She began to tremble. She was aware that they were too intent upon their business to think that any one was watching them, but she dared not move. Suddenly, rending the sultry silence of the night like a piece of silk violently torn in two, came the crowing of a cock. Mrs. Hamlyn almost shrieked. Mr. Pryce was trying to save the life of his friend and master by a sacrifice to the strange gods of the East. The voice went on, low and insistent. Then in the dark circle there was a movement, something was happening, she knew not what; there was a cluck-cluck from the cock, angry and frightened, and then a strange, indescribable sound; the magician was cutting the cock's throat; then silence; there were vague doings that she could not follow, and in a little while it looked as though some one was stamping out the fire. The figures she had dimly seen were dissolved in the night and all once more was still. She heard again the regular throbbing of the engines.

Mrs. Hamlyn stood still for a little while, strangely shaken, and then walked slowly along the deck. She found a chair and lay down in it. She was trembling still. She could only guess what had happened. She did not know how long she lay there, but at last she felt that the dawn was approaching. It was not yet day, but it was no longer night. Against the darkness of the sky she could now see the ship's rail. Then she saw a figure come towards her. It was a man in pyjamas.

"Who's that?" she cried nervously.

"Only the doctor," came a friendly voice.

"Oh! What are you doing here at this time of night?"

"I've been with Gallagher." He sat down beside her and lit a cigarette. "I've given him a good strong hypodermic and he's quiet now."

"Has he been very ill?"

"I thought he was going to pass out. I was watching him, and suddenly he started up on his bed and began to talk Malay. Of course I couldn't understand a thing. He kept on saying one word over and over again."

"Perhaps it was a name, a woman's name."

"He wanted to get out of bed. He's a damned powerful man even now. By George, I had a struggle with him. I was afraid he'd throw himself overboard. He seemed to think some one was calling him."

"When was that?" asked Mrs. Hamlyn slowly.

"Between four and half-past. Why?"

"Nothing."

She shuddered.

Later in the morning when the ship's life was set upon its daily round, Mrs. Hamlyn passed Pryce on the deck, but he gave her a brief greeting and walked on with quickly averted gaze. He looked tired and overwrought. Mrs. Hamlyn thought again of that fat woman, with golden ornaments in her thick, black hair, who sat on the steps of the deserted bungalow and looked at the road which ran through the trim lines of the rubber trees.

It was fearfully hot. She knew now why the night had been so dark. The sky was no longer blue, but a dead, level white; its surface was too even to give the effect of cloud; it was as though in the upper air the heat hung like a pall. There was no breeze and the sea, as colourless as the sky, was smooth and shining like the dye in a dyer's vat. The passengers

were listless; when they walked round the deck they
panted and beads of sweat broke out on their fore-
heads. They spoke in undertones. Something uncanny and disquieting brooded over the ship, and
they could not bring themselves to laugh. A feeling
of resentment arose in their hearts; they were alive
and well, and it exasperated them that, so near, a
man should be dying and by the fact (which was
after all no concern of theirs) so mysteriously af-
fect them. A planter in the smoking-room over a
gin sling said brutally what most of them felt, though
none had confessed.

"Well, if he's going to peg out," he said, "I wish
he'd hurry up and get it over. It gives me the
creeps."

The day was interminable. Mrs. Hamlyn was
thankful when the dinner hour arrived. So much
time, at all events, was passed. She sat at the doctor's table.

"When do we reach Aden?" she asked.

"Some time to-morrow. The captain says we shall
sight land between five and six in the morning."

She gave him a sharp look. He stared at her for
a moment, then dropped his eyes and reddened. He
remembered that the woman, the fat woman sitting
on the bungalow steps, had said that Gallagher
would never see the land. Mrs. Hamlyn wondered
whether he, the sceptical, matter-of-fact young doctor, was wavering at last. He frowned a little, and
then, as though he sought to pull himself together,
looked at her once more.

"I shan't be sorry to hand over my patient to the hospital people at Aden, I can tell you," he said.

Next day was Christmas eve. When Mrs. Hamlyn awoke from a troubled sleep the dawn was breaking. She looked out of her porthole and saw that the sky was clear and silvery; during the night the haze had melted, and the morning was brilliant. With a lighter heart she went on deck. She walked as far forward as she could go. A late star twinkled palely close to the horizon. There was a shimmer on the sea as though a loitering breeze passed playful fingers over its surface. The light was exquisitely soft, tenuous like a budding wood in spring, and crystalline so that it reminded you of the bubbling of water in a mountain brook. She turned to look at the sun rising rosy in the east, and saw coming towards her the doctor. He wore his uniform; he had not been to bed all night; he was dishevelled and he walked, with bowed shoulders, as though he were dog-tired. She knew at once that Gallagher was dead. When he came up to her she saw that he was crying. He looked so young then that her heart went out to him. She took his hand.

"You poor dear," she said. "You're tired out."

"I did all I could," he said. "I wanted so awfully to save him."

His voice shook and she saw that he was almost hysterical.

"When did he die?" she asked.

He closed his eyes, trying to control himself, and his lips trembled.

"A few minutes ago."

Mrs. Hamlyn sighed. She found nothing to say. Her gaze wandered across the calm, dispassionate and ageless sea. It stretched on all sides of them as infinite as human sorrow. But on a sudden her eyes were held, for there, ahead of them, on the horizon was something which looked like a precipitous and massy cloud. But its outline was too sharp to be a cloud's. She touched the doctor on the arm.

"What's that?"

He looked at it for a moment and under his sunburn she saw him grow white.

"Land."

Once more Mrs. Hamlyn thought of the fat Malay woman who sat silent on the steps of Gallagher's bungalow. Did she know?

They buried him when the sun was high in the heavens. They stood on the lower deck and on the hatches, the first- and second-class passengers, the white stewards and the European officers. The missionary read the burial service.

"Man that is born of woman hath but a short time to live, and is full of misery. He cometh up, and is cut down, like a flower; he fleeth as it were a shadow, and never continueth in one stay."

Pryce looked down at the deck with knit brows. His teeth were tightly clenched. He did not grieve, for his heart was hot with anger. The doctor and the consul stood side by side. The consul bore to a nicety the expression of an official regret, but the doctor, clean-shaven now, in his neat fresh uniform and his gold braid, was pale and harassed. From him Mrs. Hamlyn's eyes wandered to Mrs. Linsell. She was pressed against her husband, weeping, and he was holding her hand tenderly. Mrs. Hamlyn did not know why this sight singularly affected her. At that moment of grief, her nerves distraught, the little woman went by instinct to the protection and support of her husband. But then Mrs. Hamlyn felt a little shudder pass through her and she fixed her eyes on the seams in the deck, for she did not want to see what was toward. There was a pause in the reading. There were various movements. One of the officers gave an order. The missionary's voice continued.

"Forasmuch as it has pleased Almighty God of his great mercy to take unto himself the soul of our dear brother here departed; we therefore commend his body to the deep, to be turned into corruption, looking for the resurrection of the body when the sea shall give up its dead."

Mrs. Hamlyn felt the hot tears flow down her cheeks. There was a dull splash. The missionary's voice went on.

When the service was finished the passengers scattered; the second-class passengers returned to their quarters and a bell rang to summon them to luncheon. But the first-class passengers sauntered aimlessly about the promenade deck. Most of the men made for the smoking-room and sought to cheer themselves with whiskies and sodas and with gin slings. But the consul put up a notice on the board outside the dining-saloon summoning the passengers to a meeting. Most of them had an idea for what purpose it was called and at the appointed hour they assembled. They were more cheerful than they had been for a week and they chattered with a gaiety which was only subdued by a mannerly reserve. The consul, an eye-glass in his eye, said that he had gathered them together to discuss the question of the fancy-dress ball on the following day. He knew they all had the deepest sympathy for Mr. Gallagher and he would have proposed that they should combine to send an appropriate message to the deceased's relatives; but his papers had been examined by the purser and no trace could be found of any relative or friend with whom it was possible to communicate. The late Mr. Gallagher appeared to be quite alone in the world. Meanwhile he (the consul) ventured to offer his sincere sympathy to the doctor who, he was quite sure, had done everything that was possible in the circumstances.

"Hear, hear," said the passengers.

They had all passed through a very trying time, proceeded the consul, and to some it might seem that it would be more respectful to the deceased's memory if the fancy-dress ball were postponed till New Year's eve. This, however, he told them frankly was not his view, and he was convinced that Mr. Gallagher himself would not have wished it. Of course it was a question for the majority to decide. The doctor got up and thanked the consul and the passengers for the kind things that had been said of him, it had of course been a very trying time, but he was authorised by the captain to say that the captain expressly wished all the festivities to be carried out

on Christmas day as though nothing had happened.
He (the doctor) told them in confidence that the
captain felt the passengers had got into a rather mor-
bid state and thought it would do them all good if
they had a jolly good time on Christmas day. Then
the missionary's wife rose and said they mustn't think
only of themselves; it had been arranged by the Entertainment Committee that there should be a
Christmas tree for the children immediately after
the first-class passengers' dinner, and the children
had been looking forward to seeing every one in
fancy dress; it would be too bad to disappoint them;
she yielded to no one in her respect for the dead and
she sympathised with any one who felt too sad to
think of dancing just then. Her own heart was very
heavy, but she did feel it would be merely selfish to
give way to a feeling which could do no good to any
one. Let them think of the little ones. This very
much impressed the passengers. They wanted to
forget the brooding terror which had hung over the
boat for so many days, they were alive and they
wanted to enjoy themselves; but they had an uneasy
notion that it would be decent to exhibit a certain
grief. It was quite another matter if they could do
as they wished from altruistic motives. When the
consul called for a show of hands every one, but
Mrs. Hamlyn and one old lady who was rheumatic,
held up an eager arm.

"The ayes have it," said the consul. "And I venture to congratulate the meeting on a very sensible
decision."

It was just going to break up when one of the

planters got on his feet and said he wished to offer a
suggestion. In the circumstances didn't they all
think it would be as well to invite the second-class
passengers? They had all come to the funeral that
morning. The missionary jumped up and seconded
the motion. The events of the last few days had
drawn them all together, he said, and in the presence
of death all men were equal. The consul again addressed them. This matter had been discussed at a
previous meeting and the conclusion had been
reached that it would be pleasanter for the second-
class passengers to have their own party, but circumstances alter cases, and he was distinctly of opinion
that their previous decision should be reversed.

"Hear, hear," said the passengers.

A wave of democratic feeling swept over them
and the motion was carried by acclamation. They
separated light-heartedly, they felt charitable and
kindly. Every one stood every one else drinks in
the smoking-room. .

And so, on the following evening, Mrs. Hamlyn
put on her fancy-dress. She had no heart for the
gaiety before her, and for a moment had thought of
feigning illness, but she knew no one would believe
her, and was afraid to be thought affected. She
was dressed as Carmen and she could not resist
the vanity of making herself as attractive as possible.
She darkened her eyelashes and rouged her cheeks.
The costume suited her. When the bugle sounded
and she went into the saloon she was received with
flattering surprise. The consul (always a humour-
ist) was dressed as a ballet-girl and was greeted with

shouts of delighted laughter. The missionary and
his wife, self-conscious but pleased with themselves,
were very grand as Manchus. Mrs. Linsell, as Columbine, showed all that was possible of her very
pretty legs. Her husband was an Arab sheik and
the doctor was a Malay sultan.

A subscription had been collected to provide champagne at dinner and the meal was hilarious. The
company had provided crackers in which were paper
hats of various shapes and these the passengers put
on. There were paper streamers too which they
threw at one another and little balloons which they
beat from one to the other across the room. They
laughed and shouted. They were very gay. No one
could say that they were not having a good time. As
soon as dinner was finished they went into the saloon
where the Christmas tree, with candles lit, was
ready, and the children were brought in, shrieking
with delight, and given presents. Then the dance
began. The second-class passengers stood about
shyly round the part of the deck reserved for dancing and occasionally danced with one another.

"I'm glad we had them," said the consul, dancing
with Mrs. Hamlyn. "I'm all for democracy, and I
think they're very sensible to keep themselves to
themselves."

But she noticed that Pryce was not to be seen, and
when an opportunity presented asked one of the
second-class passengers where he was.

"Blind to the world," was the answer. "We put
him to bed in the afternoon and locked him up in his
cabin."

The consul claimed her for another dance. He was very facetious. Suddenly Mrs. Hamlyn felt that she could not bear it any more, the noise of the amateur band, the consul's jokes, the gaiety of the dancers. She knew not why, but the merriment of those people passing on their ship through the night and the solitary sea affected her on a sudden with horror. When the consul released her she slipped away and, with a look to see that no one had noticed her, ascended the companion to the boat-deck. Here everything was in darkness. She walked softly to a spot where she knew she would be safe from all intrusion. But she heard a faint laugh and she caught sight in a hidden corner of a Columbine and a Malay sultan. Mrs. Linsell and the doctor had resumed already the flirtation which the death of Gallagher had interrupted.

Already all those people had put out of their minds with a kind of ferocity the thought of that poor lonely man who had so strangely died in their midst. They felt no compassion for him, but resentment rather, because on his account they had been ill-at-ease. They seized upon life avidly. They made their jokes, they flirted, they gossiped. Mrs. Hamlyn remembered what the consul had said, that among Mr. Gallagher's papers no letter could be found, not the name of a single friend to whom the news of his death might be sent, and she knew not why this seemed to her unbearably tragic. There was something mysterious in a man who could pass through the world in such solitariness. When she remembered how he had come on deck in Singapore, so

short a while since, in such rude health, full of vitality, and his arrogant plans for the future, she was
seized with dismay. Those words of the burial service filled her with a solemn awe: *Man that is born
of woman hath but a short time to live, and is full
of misery. He cometh up, and is cut down, like a
flower.* . . . Year in, year out, he had made his
plans for the future, he wanted to live so much and
he had so much to live for, and then just when he
stretched out his hand—oh, it was pitiful; it made
all the other distresses of the world of small account. Death with its mystery was the only thing
that really mattered. Mrs. Hamlyn leaned over
the rail and looked at the starry sky. Why did
people make themselves unhappy? Let them weep
for the death of those they loved, death was terrible
always, but for the rest, was it worth while to be
wretched, to harbour malice, to be vain and unchar-
itable? She thought again of herself and her husband and the woman he so strangely loved. He too
had said that we live to be happy so short a time
and we are so long dead. She pondered long and
intently, and suddenly, as summer lightning flashes
across the darkness of the night, she made a discov-
ery which filled her with tremulous surprise; for she
found that in her heart was no longer anger with her
husband nor jealousy of her rival. A notion dawned
on some remote horizon of her consciousness and
like the morning sun suffused her soul with a tender,
blissful glow. Out of the tragedy of that unknown
Irishman's death she gathered elatedly the courage
for a desperate resolution. Her heart beat quickly,

she was impatient to carry it into effect. A passion for self-sacrifice seized her.

The music had stopped, the ball was over; most of the passengers would have gone to bed and the rest would be in the smoking-room. She went down to her cabin and met no one on the way. She took her writing-pad and wrote a letter to her husband.

My dear. It is Christmas day and I want to tell you that my heart is filled with kindly thoughts towards both of you. I have been foolish and unreasonable. I think we should allow those we care for to be happy in their own way, and we should care for them enough not to let it make us unhappy. I want you to know that I grudge you none of the joy that has so strangely come into your life. I am no longer jealous, nor hurt, nor vindictive. Do not think I shall be unhappy or lonely. If ever you feel that you need me, come to me, and I will welcome you with a cheerful spirit and without reproach or ill-will. I am most grateful for all the years of happiness and of tenderness that you gave me, and in return I wish to offer you an affection which makes no claim on you and is, I hope, utterly disinterested. Think kindly of me and be happy, happy, happy.

She signed her name and put the letter into an envelope. Though it would not go till they reached Port Said she wanted to place it at once in the letter-box. When she had done this, beginning to undress, she looked at herself in the glass. Her eyes were shining and under her rouge her colour was bright. The future was no longer desolate, but bright with a fair hope. She slipped into bed and fell at once into a sound and dreamless sleep.

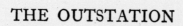

THE OUTSTATION

THE OUTSTATION

THE new assistant arrived in the afternoon. When the Resident, Mr. Warburton, was told that the prahu was in sight he put on his solar topee and went down to the landing-stage. The guard, eight little Dyak soldiers, stood to attention as he passed. He noted with satisfaction that their bearing was martial, their uniforms neat and clean, and their guns shining. They were a credit to him. From the landing-stage he watched the bend of the river round which in a moment the boat would sweep. He looked very smart in his spotless ducks and white shoes. He held under his arm a gold-headed Malacca cane which had been given him by the Sultan of Perak. He awaited the newcomer with mingled feelings. There was more work in the district than one man could properly do, and during his periodical tours of the country under his charge it had been inconvenient to leave the station in the hands of a native clerk, but he had been so long the only white man there that he could not face the arrival of another without misgiving. He was accustomed to loneliness. During the war he had not seen an English face for three years; and once when he was instructed to put up an afforestation officer he was seized with panic, so that when the stranger was due to arrive, having arranged everything for his reception, he wrote a note telling him he was obliged to go up-river, and fled; he remained away till he was informed by a messenger that his guest had left.

Now the prahu appeared in the broad reach. It was manned by prisoners, Dyaks under various sentences, and a couple of warders were waiting on the landing-stage to take them back to jail. They were sturdy fellows, used to the river, and they rowed with a powerful stroke. As the boat reached the side a man got out from under the attap awning and stepped on shore. The guard presented arms.

"Here we are at last. By God, I'm as cramped as the devil. I've brought you your mail."

He spoke with exuberant joviality. Mr. Warburton politely held out his hand.

"Mr. Cooper, I presume?"

"That's right. Were you expecting any one else?"

The question had a facetious intent, but the Resident did not smile.

"My name is Warburton. I'll show you your quarters. They'll bring your kit along."

He preceded Cooper along the narrow pathway and they entered a compound in which stood a small bungalow.

"I've had it made as habitable as I could, but of course no one has lived in it for a good many years."

It was built on piles. It consisted of a long living-room which opened on to a broad verandah, and behind, on each side of a passage, were two bed-rooms.

"This'll do me all right," said Cooper.

"I daresay you want to have a bath and a change. I shall be very much pleased if you'll dine with me to-night. Will eight o'clock suit you?"

"Any old time will do for me."

The Resident gave a polite, but slightly discon-certed, smile and withdrew. He returned to the Fort where his own residence was. The impression which Allen Cooper had given him was not very fa-vourable, but he was a fair man, and he knew that it was unjust to form an opinion on so brief a glimpse. Cooper seemed to be about thirty. He was a tall, thin fellow, with a sallow face in which there was not a spot of colour. It was a face all in one tone. He had a large, hooked nose and blue eyes. When, entering the bungalow, he had taken off his topee and flung it to a waiting boy, Mr. War-burton noticed that his large skull, covered with short, brown hair, contrasted somewhat oddly with a weak, small chin. He was dressed in khaki shorts and a khaki shirt, but they were shabby and soiled; and his battered topee had not been cleaned for days. Mr. Warburton reflected that the young man had spent a week on a coasting steamer and had passed the last forty-eight hours lying in the bottom of a prahu.

"We'll see what he looks like when he comes in to dinner."

He went into his room where his things were as neatly laid out as if he had an English valet, undressed, and, walking down the stairs to the bath-house, sluiced himself with cool water. The only concession he made to the climate was to wear a white dinner-jacket; but otherwise, in a boiled shirt and a high collar, silk socks and patent-leather shoes, he dressed as formally as though he were dining at his club in Pall Mall. A careful host, he went into the dining-room to see that the table was properly laid. It was gay with orchids and the silver shone brightly. The napkins were folded into elaborate shapes. Shaded candles in silver candlesticks shed a soft light. Mr. Warburton smiled his approval and returned to the sitting-room to await his guest. Presently he appeared. Cooper was wearing the khaki shorts, the khaki shirt, and the ragged jacket in which he had landed. Mr. Warburton's smile of greeting froze on his face.

"Hulloa, you're all dressed up," said Cooper. "I didn't know you were going to do that. I very nearly put on a sarong."

"It doesn't matter at all. I daresay your boys were busy."

"You needn't have bothered to dress on my account, you know."

"I didn't. I always dress for dinner."

"Even when you're alone?"

"Especially when I'm alone," replied Mr. Warburton, with a frigid stare.

He saw a twinkle of amusement in Cooper's eyes, and he flushed an angry red. Mr. Warburton was a hot-tempered man; you might have guessed that from his red face with its pugnacious features and from his red hair, now growing white; his blue eyes, cold as a rule and observing, could flush with sudden wrath; but he was a man of the world and he hoped a just one. He must do his best to get on with this fellow.

"When I lived in London I moved in circles in which it would have been just as eccentric not to dress for dinner every night as not to have a bath every morning. When I came to Borneo I saw no reason to discontinue so good a habit. For three years, during the war, I never saw a white man. I never omitted to dress on a single occasion on which I was well enough to come in to dinner. You have not been very long in this country; believe me, there is no better way to maintain the proper pride which you should have in yourself. When a white man surrenders in the slightest degree to the influences that surround him he very soon loses his self-respect, and when he loses his self-respect you may be quite sure that the natives will soon cease to respect him."

"Well, if you expect me to put on a boiled shirt and a stiff collar in this heat I'm afraid you'll be disappointed."

"When you are dining in your own bungalow you will, of course, dress as you think fit, but when you do me the pleasure of dining with me, perhaps you will come to the conclusion that it is only polite to wear the costume usual in civilised society."

Two Malay boys, in sarongs and songkoks, with smart white coats and brass buttons, came in, one bearing gin pahits, and the other a tray on which were olives and anchovies. Then they went in to dinner. Mr. Warburton flattered himself that he had the best cook, a Chinese, in Borneo, and he took great trouble to have as good food as in the difficult circumstances was possible. He exercised much ingenuity in making the best of his materials.

"Would you care to look at the menu?" he said, handing it to Cooper.

It was written in French and the dishes had resounding names. They were waited on by the two boys. In opposite corners of the room two more waved immense fans, and so gave movement to the sultry air. The fare was sumptuous and the champagne excellent.

"Do you do yourself like this every day?" said Cooper.

Mr. Warburton gave the menu a careless glance.

"I have not noticed that the dinner is any different from usual," he said. "I eat very little myself, but I make a point of having a proper dinner served to me every night. It keeps the cook in practice and it's good discipline for the boys."

The conversation proceeded with effort. Mr. Warburton was elaborately courteous, and it may be that he found a slightly malicious amusement in the embarrassment which he thereby occasioned in his companion. Cooper had not been more than a few months in Sembulu, and Mr. Warburton's enquiries about friends of his in Kuala Solor were soon exhausted.

"By the way," he said presently, "did you meet a lad called Hennerley? He's come out recently, I believe."

"Oh, yes, he's in the police. A rotten bounder."

"I should hardly have expected him to be that. His uncle is my friend Lord Barraclough. I had a letter from Lady Barraclough only the other day asking me to look out for him."

"I heard he was related to somebody or other. I suppose that's how he got the job. He's been to Eton and Oxford and he doesn't forget to let you know it."

"You surprise me," said Mr. Warburton. "All his family have been at Eton and Oxford for a couple of hundred years. I should have expected him to take it as a matter of course."

"I thought him a damned prig."

"To what school did you go?"

"I was born in Barbadoes. I was educated there."

"Oh, I see."

Mr. Warburton managed to put so much offensiveness into his brief reply that Cooper flushed. For a moment he was silent.

"I've had two or three letters from Kuala Solor," continued Mr. Warburton, "and my impression was that young Hennerley was a great success. They say he's a first-rate sportsman."

"Oh, yes, he's very popular. He's just the sort of fellow they would like in K.S. I haven't got much use for the first-rate sportsman myself. What does it amount to in the long run that a man can play golf and tennis better than other people? And who cares if he can make a break of seventy-five at billiards? They attach a damned sight too much importance to that sort of thing in England."

"Do you think so? I was under the impression that the first-rate sportsman had come out of the war certainly no worse than any one else."

"Oh, if you're going to talk of the war then I do know what I'm talking about. I was in the same regiment as Hennerley and I can tell you that the men couldn't stick him at any price."

"How do you know?"

"Because I was one of the men."

"Oh, you hadn't got a commission."

"A fat chance I had of getting a commission. I was what was called a Colonial. I hadn't been to a public school and I had no influence. I was in the ranks the whole damned time."

Cooper frowned. He seemed to have difficulty in preventing himself from breaking into violent invective. Mr. Warburton watched him, his little blue eyes narrowed, watched him and formed his opinion. Changing the conversation, he began to speak to Cooper about the work that would be required of him, and as the clock struck ten he rose.

"Well, I won't keep you any more. I daresay you're tired by your journey."

They shook hands.

"Oh, I say, look here," said Cooper, "I wonder if you can find me a boy. The boy I had before never turned up when I was starting from K.S. He took my kit on board and all that and then disappeared. I didn't know he wasn't there till we were out of the river."

"I'll ask my head-boy. I have no doubt he can find you some one."

"All right. Just tell him to send the boy along and if I like the look of him I'll take him."

There was a moon, so that no lantern was needed. Cooper walked across from the Fort to his bungalow.

"I wonder why on earth they've sent me a fellow like that?" reflected Mr. Warburton. "If that's the kind of man they're going to get out now I don't think much of it."

He strolled down his garden. The Fort was built on the top of a little hill and the garden ran down to the river's edge; on the bank was an arbour, and hither it was his habit to come after dinner to smoke a cheroot. And often from the river that flowed below him a voice was heard, the voice of some Malay too timorous to venture into the light of day, and a complaint or an accusation was softly wafted to his ears, a piece of information was whispered to him or a useful hint, which otherwise would never have come into his official ken. He threw himself heavily into a long rattan chair. Cooper! An envious, ill-bred fellow, bumptious, self-assertive and vain. But Mr. Warburton's irritation could not withstand the silent beauty of the night. The air was scented with the sweet-smelling flowers of a tree that grew at the entrance to the arbour, and the fireflies, sparkling dimly, flew with their slow and silvery flight. The moon made a pathway on the broad river for the light feet of Siva's bride, and on the further bank a row of palm trees was delicately silhouetted against the sky. Peace stole into the soul of Mr. Warburton.

He was a queer creature and he had had a singular career. At the age of twenty-one he had inherited a considerable fortune, a hundred thousand pounds, and when he left Oxford he threw himself into the gay life which in those days (now Mr. Warburton was a man of four and fifty) offered itself to the young man of good family. He had his flat in Mount Street, his private hansom, and his hunting-box in Warwickshire. He went to all the places where the fashionable congregate. He was handsome, amusing and generous. He was a figure in the society of London in the early nineties, and society then had not lost its exclusiveness nor its brilliance. The Boer War which shook it was unthought of; the Great War which destroyed it was prophesied only by the pessimists. It was no unpleasant thing to be a rich young man in those days, and Mr. Warburton's chimney-piece during the season was packed with cards for one great function after another. Mr. Warburton displayed them with complacency. For Mr. Warburton was a snob. He was not a timid snob, a little ashamed of being impressed by his betters, nor a snob who sought the intimacy of persons who had acquired celebrity in politics or notoriety in the arts, nor the snob who was dazzled by riches; he was the naked, unadulterated common snob who dearly loved a lord. He was touchy and quick-tempered, but he would much rather have been snubbed by a person of quality than flattered by a commoner. His name figured insignificantly in Burke's Peerage, and it was marvellous to watch the

ingenuity he used to mention his distant relationship
to the noble family he belonged to; but never a word
did he say of the honest Liverpool manufacturer
from whom, through his mother, a Miss Gubbins, he
had come by his fortune. It was the terror of his
fashionable life that at Cowes, maybe, or at Ascot,
when he was with a duchess or even with a prince of
the blood, one of these relatives would claim
acquaintance with him.

His failing was too obvious not soon to become
notorious, but its extravagance saved it from being
merely despicable. The great whom he adored
laughed at him, but in their hearts felt his adora-
tion not unnatural. Poor Warburton was a dreadful snob, of course, but after all he was a good fellow. He was always ready to back a bill for an
impecunious nobleman, and if you were in a tight
corner you could safely count on him for a hundred
pounds. He gave good dinners. He played whist
badly, but never minded how much he lost if the
company was select. He happened to be a gambler,
an unlucky one, but he was a good loser, and it was
impossible not to admire the coolness with which he
lost five hundred pounds at a sitting. His passion
for cards, almost as strong as his passion for titles,
was the cause of his undoing. The life he led was
expensive and his gambling losses were formidable.
He began to plunge more heavily, first on horses,
and then on the Stock Exchange. He had a certain
simplicity of character and the unscrupulous found
him an ingenuous prey. I do not know if he ever
realised that his smart friends laughed at him behind

his back, but I think he had an obscure instinct that he could not afford to appear other than careless of his money. He got into the hands of money-lenders. At the age of thirty-four he was ruined.

He was too much imbued with the spirit of his class to hesitate in the choice of his next step. When a man in his set had run through his money he went out to the colonies. No one heard Mr. Warburton repine. He made no complaint because a noble friend had advised a disastrous speculation, he pressed nobody to whom he had lent money to repay it, he paid his debts (if he had only known it, the despised blood of the Liverpool manufacturer came out in him there), sought help from no one, and, never having done a stroke of work in his life, looked for a means of livelihood. He remained cheerful, unconcerned and full of humour. He had no wish to make any one with whom he happened to be uncomfortable by the recital of his misfortune. Mr. Warburton was a snob, but he was also a gentleman.

The only favour he asked of any of the great friends in whose daily company he had lived for years was a recommendation. The able man who was at that time Sultan of Sembulu took him into his service. The night before he sailed he dined for the last time at his club.

"I hear you're going away, Warburton," the old Duke of Hereford said to him.

"Yes, I'm going to Borneo."

"Good God, what are you going there for?"

"Oh, I'm broke."

"Are you? I'm sorry. Well, let us know when you come back. I hope you have a good time."

"Oh, yes. Lots of shooting, you know."

The Duke nodded and passed on. A few hours later Mr. Warburton watched the coast of England recede into the mist, and he left behind everything which to him made life worth living.

Twenty years had passed since then. He kept up a busy correspondence with various great ladies and his letters were amusing and chatty. He never lost his love for titled persons and paid careful attention to the announcements in The Times (which reached him six weeks after publication) of their comings and goings. He perused the column which records births, deaths, and marriages, and he was always ready with his letter of congratulation or condolence. The illustrated papers told him how people looked and on his periodical visits to England, able to take up the threads as though they had never been broken, he knew all about any new person who might have appeared on the social surface. His interest in the world of fashion was as vivid as when himself had been a figure in it. It still seemed to him the only thing that mattered.

But insensibly another interest had entered into his life. The position he found himself in flattered his vanity; he was no longer the sycophant craving the smiles of the great, he was the master whose word was law. He was gratified by the guard of Dyak soldiers who presented arms as he passed. He liked to sit in judgment on his fellow men. It pleased him to compose quarrels between rival chiefs. When the head-hunters were troublesome in the old days he set out to chastise them with a thrill of pride in his own behaviour. He was too vain not to be of dauntless courage, and a pretty story was told of his coolness in adventuring single-handed into a stockaded village and demanding the surrender of a bloodthirsty pirate. He became a skilful administrator. He was strict, just and honest.

And little by little he conceived a deep love for the Malays. He interested himself in their habits and customs. He was never tired of listening to their talk. He admired their virtues, and with a smile and a shrug of the shoulders condoned their vices.

"In my day," he would say, "I have been on intimate terms with some of the greatest gentlemen in England, but I have never known finer gentlemen than some well-born Malays whom I am proud to call my friends."

He liked their courtesy and their distinguished manners, their gentleness and their sudden passions. He knew by instinct exactly how to treat them. He had a genuine tenderness for them. But he never forgot that he was an English gentleman and he had no patience with the white men who yielded to native customs. He made no surrenders. And he did not imitate so many of the white men in taking a native woman to wife, for an intrigue of this nature, however sanctified by custom, seemed to him not only shocking but undignified. A man who had been called George by Albert Edward, Prince of Wales, could hardly be expected to have any connection with a native. And when he returned to Borneo from his visits to England it was now with something like relief. His friends, like himself, were no longer young, and there was a new generation which looked upon him as a tiresome old man. It seemed to him that the England of to-day had lost a good deal of what he had loved in the England of his youth. But Borneo remained the same. It was home to him now. He meant to remain in the service as long as was possible, and the hope in his heart was that he would die before at last he was forced to retire. He had stated in his will that wherever he died he wished his body to be brought back to Sembulu and buried among the people he loved within sound of the softly flowing river.

But these emotions he kept hidden from the eyes of men; and no one, seeing this spruce, stout, well-set-up man, with his clean-shaven strong face and his whitening hair, would have dreamed that he cherished so profound a sentiment.

He knew how the work of the station should be done, and during the next few days he kept a suspicious eye on his assistant. He saw very soon that he was painstaking and competent. The only fault he had to find with him was that he was brusque with the natives.

"The Malays are shy and very sensitive," he said to him. "I think you will find that you will get much better results if you take care always to be polite, patient and kindly."

Cooper gave a short, grating laugh.

"I was born in Barbadoes and I was in Africa in the war. I don't think there's much about niggers that I don't know."

"I know nothing," said Mr. Warburton acidly. "But we were not talking of them. We were talking of Malays."

"Aren't they niggers?"

"You are very ignorant," replied Mr. Warburton. He said no more.

On the first Sunday after Cooper's arrival he asked him to dinner. He did everything ceremoniously, and though they had met on the previous day in the office and later, on the Fort verandah where they drank a gin and bitters together at six o'clock, he sent a polite note across to the bungalow by a boy. Cooper, however unwillingly, came in evening dress and Mr. Warburton, though gratified that his wish was respected, noticed with disdain that the young man's clothes were badly cut and his shirt ill-fitting. But Mr. Warburton was in a good temper that evening.

"By the way," he said to him, as he shook hands, "I've talked to my head-boy about finding you some one and he recommends his nephew. I've seen him and he seems a bright and willing lad. Would you like to see him?"

"I don't mind."

"He's waiting now."

Mr. Warburton called his boy and told him to send for his nephew. In a moment a tall, slender youth of twenty appeared. He had large dark eyes and a good profile. He was very neat in his sarong, a little white coat, and a fez, without a tassel, of plum-coloured velvet. He answered to the name of Abas. Mr. Warburton looked on him with approval, and his manner insensibly softened as he spoke to him in fluent and idiomatic Malay. He was inclined to be sarcastic with white people, but with the Malays he had a happy mixture of condescension and kindliness. He stood in the place of the Sultan. He knew perfectly how to preserve his own dignity, and at the same time put a native at his ease.

"Will he do?" said Mr. Warburton, turning to Cooper.

"Yes, I daresay he's no more of a scoundrel than any of the rest of them."

Mr. Warburton informed the boy that he was engaged and dismissed him.

"You're very lucky to get a boy like that," he told Cooper. "He belongs to a very good family. They came over from Malacca nearly a hundred years ago."

"I don't much mind if the boy who cleans my shoes and brings me a drink when I want it has blue blood in his veins or not. All I ask is that he should do what I tell him and look sharp about it."

Mr. Warburton pursed his lips, but made no reply.

They went in to dinner. It was excellent, and the wine was good. Its influence presently had its effect on them and they talked not only without acrimony, but even with friendliness. Mr. Warburton liked to do himself well, and on Sunday night he made it a habit to do himself even a little better than usual. He began to think he was unfair to Cooper. Of course he was not a gentleman, but that was not his fault, and when you got to know him it might be that he would turn out a very good fellow. His faults, perhaps, were faults of manner. And he was certainly good at his work, quick, conscientious and thorough. When they reached the dessert Mr. Warburton was feeling kindly disposed towards all mankind.

"This is your first Sunday and I'm going to give you a very special glass of port. I've only got about two dozen of it left and I keep it for special occasions."

He gave his boy instructions and presently the bottle was brought. Mr. Warburton watched the boy open it.

"I got this port from my old friend Charles Hollington. He'd had it for forty years and I've had it for a good many. He was well known to have the best cellar in England."

"Is he a wine merchant?"

"Not exactly," smiled Mr. Warburton. "I was speaking of Lord Hollington of Castle Reagh. He's one of the richest peers in England. A very old friend of mine. I was at Eton with his brother."

This was an opportunity that Mr. Warburton could never resist and he told a little anecdote of which the only point seemed to be that he knew an earl. The port was certainly very good; he drank a glass and then a second. He lost all caution. He

had not talked to a white man for months. He
began to tell stories. He showed himself in the
company of the great. Hearing him you would have
thought that at one time ministries were formed
and policies decided on his suggestion whispered into
the ear of a duchess or thrown over the dinner-table
to be gratefully acted on by the confidential adviser
of the sovereign. The old days at Ascot, Goodwood
and Cowes lived again for him. Another glass of
port. There were the great house-parties in Yorkshire and in Scotland to which he went every year.

"I had a man called Foreman then, the best valet
I ever had, and why do you think he gave me notice?
You know in the Housekeeper's Room the ladies'
maids and the gentlemen's gentlemen sit according to
the precedence of their masters. He told me he was
sick of going to party after party at which I was
the only commoner. It meant that he always had
to sit at the bottom of the table and all the best
bits were taken before a dish reached him. I told
the story to the old Duke of Hereford and he
roared. 'By God, sir,' he said, 'if I were King of
England I'd make you a viscount just to give your
man a chance.' 'Take him yourself, Duke,' I said.
'He's the best valet I've ever had.' 'Well, Warburton,' he said, 'if he's good enough for you he's good
enough for me. Send him along.' "

Then there was Monte Carlo where Mr. Warburton and the Grand Duke Fyodor, playing in partner-
ship, had broken the bank one evening; and there
was Marienbad. At Marienbad Mr. Warburton
had played baccarat with Edward VII.

"He was only Prince of Wales then, of course. I remember him saying to me, 'George, if you draw on a five you'll lose your shirt.' He was right; I don't think he ever said a truer word in his life. He was a wonderful man. I always said he was the greatest diplomatist in Europe. But I was a young fool in those days, I hadn't the sense to take his advice. If I had, if I'd never drawn on a five, I daresay I shouldn't be here to-day."

Cooper was watching him. His brown eyes, deep in their sockets, were hard and supercilious, and on his lips was a mocking smile. He had heard a good deal about Mr. Warburton in Kuala Solor. Not a bad sort, and he ran his district like clockwork, they said, but by heaven, what a snob! They laughed at him good-naturedly, for it was impossible to dislike a man who was so generous and so kindly, and Cooper had already heard the story of the Prince of Wales and the game of baccarat. But Cooper listened without indulgence. From the beginning he had resented the Resident's manner. He was very sensitive and he writhed under Mr. Warburton's polite sarcasms. Mr. Warburton had a knack of receiving a remark of which he disapproved with a devastating silence. Cooper had lived little in England and he had a peculiar dislike of the English. He resented especially the public-school boy since he always feared that he was going to patronise him. He was so much afraid of others putting on airs with him that, in order as it were to get in first, he put on such airs as to make every one think him insufferably conceited.

"Well, at all events the war has done one good thing for us," he said at last. "It's smashed up the power of the aristocracy. The Boer War started it, and 1914 put the lid on."

"The great families of England are doomed," said Mr. Warburton with the complacent melancholy of an *émigré* who remembered the court of Louis XV. "They cannot afford any longer to live in their splendid palaces and their princely hospitality will soon be nothing but a memory."

"And a damned good job too in my opinion."

"My poor Cooper, what can you know of the glory that was Greece and the grandeur that was Rome?"

Mr. Warburton made an ample gesture. His eyes for an instant grew dreamy with a vision of the past.

"Well, believe me, we're fed up with all that rot. What we want is a business government by business men. I was born in a Crown Colony and I've lived practically all my life in the colonies. I don't give a row of pins for a lord. What's wrong with England is snobbishness. And if there's anything that gets my goat it's a snob."

A snob! Mr. Warburton's face grew purple and his eyes blazed with anger. That was a word that had pursued him all his life. The great ladies whose society he had enjoyed in his youth were not inclined to look upon his appreciation of themselves as unworthy, but even great ladies are sometimes out of temper and more than once Mr. Warburton had had the dreadful word flung in his teeth. He knew, he could not help knowing, that there were odious people who called him a snob. How unfair it was! Why, there was no vice he found so detestable as snobbishness. After all, he liked to mix with people of his own class, he was only at home in their company, and how in heaven's name could any one say that was snobbish? Birds of a feather.

"I quite agree with you," he answered. "A snob is a man who admires or despises another because he is of a higher social rank than his own. It is the most vulgar failing of our English middle class."

He saw a flicker of amusement in Cooper's eyes. Cooper put up his hand to hide the broad smile that rose to his lips, and so made it more noticeable. Mr. Warburton's hands trembled a little.

Probably Cooper never knew how greatly he had offended his chief. A sensitive man himself he was strangely insensitive to the feelings of others.

Their work forced them to see one another for a few minutes now and then during the day, and they met at six to have a drink on Mr. Warburton's verandah. This was an old-established custom of the country which Mr. Warburton would not for the world have broken. But they ate their meals separately, Cooper in his bungalow and Mr. Warburton at the Fort. After the office work was over they walked till dusk fell, but they walked apart. There were but few paths in this country, where the jungle pressed close upon the plantations of the village, and when Mr. Warburton caught sight of his assistant passing along with his loose stride, he would make a circuit in order to avoid him. Cooper, with his bad manners, his conceit in his own judgment and his intolerance, had already got on his nerves; but it was not till Cooper had been on the station for a couple of months that an incident happened which turned the Resident's dislike into bitter hatred.

Mr. Warburton was obliged to go up-country on a tour of inspection, and he left the station in Cooper's charge with more confidence, since he had definitely come to the conclusion that he was a capable fellow. The only thing he did not like was that he had no indulgence. He was honest, just and painstaking, but he had no sympathy for the natives. It bitterly amused Mr. Warburton to observe that this man, who looked upon himself as every man's equal, should look upon so many men as his own inferiors. He was hard, he had no patience with the native mind, and he was a bully. Mr. Warburton very quickly realised that the Malays disliked and feared him. He was not altogether displeased. He would not have liked it very much if his assistant had enjoyed a popularity which might rival his own. Mr. Warburton made his elaborate preparations, set out on his expedition, and in three weeks returned. Meanwhile the mail had arrived. The first thing that struck his eyes when he entered his sitting-room was a great pile of open newspapers. Cooper had met him, and they went into the room together. Mr. Warburton turned to one of the servants who had been left behind and sternly asked him what was the meaning of those open papers. Cooper hastened to explain.

"I wanted to read all about the Wolverhampton murder and so I borrowed your Times. I brought them back again. I knew you wouldn't mind."

Mr. Warburton turned on him, white with anger.

"But I do mind. I mind very much."

"I'm sorry," said Cooper, with composure. "The fact is, I simply couldn't wait till you came back."

"I wonder you didn't open my letters as well."

Cooper, unmoved, smiled at his chief's exasperation.

"Oh, that's not quite the same thing. After all, I couldn't imagine you'd mind my looking at your newspapers. There's nothing private in them."

"I very much object to any one reading my paper before me." He went up to the pile. There were nearly thirty numbers there. "I think it extremely impertinent of you. They're all mixed up."

"We can easily put them in order," said Cooper, joining him at the table.

"Don't touch them," cried Mr. Warburton.

"I say, it's childish to make a scene about a little thing like that."

"How dare you speak to me like that?"

"Oh, go to hell," said Cooper, and he flung out of the room.

Mr. Warburton, trembling with passion, was left contemplating his papers. His greatest pleasure in life had been destroyed by those callous, brutal hands. Most people living in out-of-the-way places when the mail comes tear open impatiently their papers and taking the last ones first glance at the latest news from home. Not so Mr. Warburton.

His newsagent had instructions to write on the outside of the wrapper the date of each paper he despatched and when the great bundle arrived Mr. Warburton looked at these dates and with his blue pencil numbered them. His head-boy's orders were to place one on the table every morning in the verandah with the early cup of tea, and it was Mr. Warburton's especial delight to break the wrapper as he sipped his tea, and read the morning paper. It gave him the illusion of living at home. Every Monday morning he read the Monday Times of six weeks back and so went through the week. On Sunday he read The Observer. Like his habit of dressing for dinner it was a tie to civilisation. And it was his pride that no matter how exciting the news was he had never yielded to the temptation of opening a paper before its allotted time. During the war the suspense sometimes had been intolerable, and when he read one day that a push was begun he had undergone agonies of suspense which he might have saved himself by the simple expedient of opening a later paper which lay waiting for him on a shelf. It had been the severest trial to which he had ever exposed himself, but he victoriously surmounted it. And that clumsy fool had broken open those neat tight packages because he wanted to know whether some horrid woman had murdered her odious husband.

Mr. Warburton sent for his boy and told him to bring wrappers. He folded up the papers as neatly as he could, placed a wrapper round each and numbered it. But it was a melancholy task.

"I shall never forgive him," he said. "Never."

Of course his boy had been with him on his expedition; he never travelled without him, for his boy knew exactly how he liked things, and Mr. Warburton was not the kind of jungle traveller who was prepared to dispense with his comforts; but in the interval since their arrival he had been gossiping in the servants' quarters. He had learnt that Cooper had had trouble with his boys. All but the youth Abas had left him. Abas had desired to go too, but his uncle had placed him there on the instructions of the Resident, and he was afraid to leave without his uncle's permission.

"I told him he had done well, Tuan," said the boy. "But he is unhappy. He says it is not a good house and he wishes to know if he may go as the others have gone."

"No, he must stay. The tuan must have servants. Have those who went been replaced?"

"No, Tuan, no one will go."

Mr. Warburton frowned. Cooper was an insolent fool, but he had an official position and must be suitably provided with servants. It was not seemly that his house should be improperly conducted.

"Where are the boys who ran away?"

"They are in the kampong, Tuan."

"Go and see them to-night and tell them that I expect them to be back in Tuan Cooper's house at dawn to-morrow."

"They say they will not go, Tuan."

"On my order?"

The boy had been with Mr. Warburton for fifteen

years, and he knew every intonation of his master's voice. He was not afraid of him, they had gone through too much together, once in the jungle the Resident had saved his life and once, upset in some rapids, but for him the Resident would have been drowned; but he knew when the Resident must be obeyed without question.

"I will go to the kampong," he said.

Mr. Warburton expected that his subordinate would take the first opportunity to apologise for his rudeness, but Cooper had the ill-bred man's inability to express regret; and when they met next morning in the office he ignored the incident. Since Mr. Warburton had been away for three weeks it was necessary for them to have a somewhat prolonged interview. At the end of it Mr. Warburton dismissed him.

"I don't think there's anything else, thank you." Cooper turned to go, but Mr. Warburton stopped him. "I understand you've been having some trouble with your boys."

Cooper gave a harsh laugh.

"They tried to blackmail me. They had the damned cheek to run away, all except that incompetent fellow Abas—he knew when he was well off—but I just sat tight. They've all come to heel again."

"What do you mean by that?"

"This morning they were all back on their jobs, the Chinese cook and all. There they were, as cool as cucumbers; you would have thought they owned the place. I suppose they'd come to the conclusion that I wasn't such a fool as I looked."

"By no means. They came back on my express order."

Cooper flushed slightly.

"I should be obliged if you wouldn't interfere with my private concerns."

"They're not your private concerns. When your servants run away it makes you ridiculous. You are perfectly free to make a fool of yourself, but I cannot allow you to be made a fool of. It is unseemly that your house should not be properly staffed. As soon as I heard that your boys had left you, I had them told to be back in their places at dawn. That'll do."

Mr. Warburton nodded to signify that the interview was at an end. Cooper took no notice.

"Shall I tell you what I did? I called them and gave the whole bally lot the sack. I gave them ten minutes to get out of the compound."

Mr. Warburton shrugged his shoulders.

"What makes you think you can get others?"

"I've told my own clerk to see about it."

Mr. Warburton reflected for a moment.

"I think you behaved very foolishly. You will do well to remember in future that good masters make good servants."

"Is there anything else you want to teach me?"

"I should like to teach you manners, but it would be an arduous task, and I have not the time to waste. I will see that you get boys."

"Please don't put yourself to any trouble on my account. I'm quite capable of getting them for myself."

Mr. Warburton smiled acidly. He had an inkling that Cooper disliked him as much as he disliked Cooper, and he knew that nothing is more galling than to be forced to accept the favours of a man you detest.

"Allow me to tell you that you have no more chance of getting Malay or Chinese servants here now than you have of getting an English butler or a French chef. No one will come to you except on an order from me. Would you like me to give it?"

"No."

"As you please. Good morning."

Mr. Warburton watched the development of the situation with acrid humour. Cooper's clerk was unable to persuade Malay, Dyak or Chinese to enter the house of such a master. Abas, the boy who remained faithful to him, knew how to cook only native food, and Cooper, a coarse feeder, found his gorge rise against the everlasting rice. There was no water-carrier, and in that great heat he needed several baths a day. He cursed Abas, but Abas opposed him with sullen resistance and would not do more than he chose. It was galling to know that the lad stayed with him only because the Resident insisted. This went on for a fortnight and then, one morning, he found in his house the very servants whom he had previously dismissed. He fell into a violent rage, but he had learnt a little sense, and this time, without a word, he let them stay. He swallowed his humiliation, but the impatient contempt he had felt for Mr. Warburton's idiosyncrasies changed into a sullen hatred; the Resident with this malicious stroke had made him the laughing-stock of all the natives.

The two men now held no communication with one another. They broke the time-honoured custom of sharing, notwithstanding personal dislike, a drink at six o'clock with any white man who happened to be at the station. Each lived in his own house as though the other did not exist. Now that Cooper had fallen into the work, it was necessary for them to have little to do with one another in the office. Mr. Warburton used his orderly to send any message he had to give his assistant, and his instructions he sent by formal letter. They saw one another constantly, that was inevitable, but did not exchange half a dozen words in a week. The fact that they could not avoid catching sight of one another got on their nerves. They brooded over their antagonism and Mr. Warburton, taking his daily walk, could think of nothing but how much he detested his assistant.

And the dreadful thing was that in all probability they would remain thus, facing each other in deadly enmity, till Mr. Warburton went on leave. It might be three years. He had no reason to send in a complaint to headquarters: Cooper did his work very well, and at that time men were hard to get. True, vague complaints reached him and hints that the natives found Cooper harsh. There was certainly a feeling of dissatisfaction among them. But when Mr. Warburton looked into specific cases, all he could say was that Cooper had shown severity where mildness would not have been misplaced and had

been unfeeling when himself would have been
sympathetic. He had done nothing for which he
could be taken to task. But Mr. Warburton watched
him. Hatred will often make a man clear-sighted,
and he had a suspicion that Cooper was using the
natives without consideration, yet keeping within the
law, because he felt that thus he could exasperate
his chief. One day perhaps he would go too far.
None knew better than Mr. Warburton how irritable the incessant heat could make a man and how
difficult it was to keep one's self-control after a
sleepless night. He smiled softly to himself.
Sooner or later Cooper would deliver himself into
his hand.

When at last the opportunity came Mr. Warburton laughed aloud. Cooper had charge of the prisoners; they made roads, built sheds, rowed when it
was necessary to send the prahu up- or down-stream,
kept the town clean and otherwise usefully employed
themselves. If well-behaved they even on occasion
served as house-boys. Cooper kept them hard at it.
He liked to see them work. He took pleasure in
devising tasks for them; and seeing quickly enough
that they were being made to do useless things the
prisoners worked badly. He punished them by
lengthening their hours. This was contrary to the
regulations, and as soon as it was brought to the attention of Mr. Warburton, without referring the
matter back to his subordinate, he gave instructions
that the old hours should be kept; Cooper, going
out for his walk, was astounded to see the prisoners
strolling back to the jail; he had given instructions

that they were not to knock off till dusk. When he asked the warder in charge why they had left off work he was told that it was the Resident's bidding.

White with rage he strode to the Fort. Mr. Warburton, in his spotless white ducks and his neat topee, with a walking-stick in his hand, followed by his dogs, was on the point of starting out on his afternoon stroll. He had watched Cooper go and knew that he had taken the road by the river. Cooper jumped up the steps and went straight up to the Resident.

"I want to know what the hell you mean by countermanding my order that the prisoners were to work till six," he burst out, beside himself with fury.

Mr. Warburton opened his cold blue eyes very wide and assumed an expression of great surprise.

"Are you out of your mind? Are you so ignorant that you do not know that that is not the way to speak to your official superior?"

"Oh, go to hell. The prisoners are my pidgin and you've got no right to interfere. You mind your business and I'll mind mine. I want to know what the devil you mean by making a damned fool of me. Every one in the place will know that you've countermanded my order."

Mr. Warburton kept very cool.

"You had no power to give the order you did. I countermanded it because it was harsh and tyrannical. Believe me, I have not made half such a damned fool of you as you have made of yourself."

"You disliked me from the first moment I came here. You've done everything you could to make the place impossible for me because I wouldn't lick your boots for you. You got your knife into me because I wouldn't flatter you."

Cooper, spluttering with rage, was nearing dangerous ground, and Mr. Warburton's eyes grew on a sudden colder and more piercing.

"You are wrong. I thought you were a cad, but I was perfectly satisfied with the way you did your work."

"You snob. You damned snob. You thought me a cad because I hadn't been to Eton. Oh, they told me in K.S. what to expect. Why, don't you know that you're the laughing-stock of the whole country? I could hardly help bursting into a roar of laughter when you told your celebrated story about the Prince of Wales. My God, how they shouted at the club when they told it. By God, I'd rather be the cad I am than the snob you are."

He got Mr. Warburton on the raw.

"If you don't get out of my house this minute I shall knock you down," he cried.

The other came a little closer to him and put his face in his.

"Touch me, touch me," he said. "By God, I'd like to see you hit me. Do you want me to say it again? Snob. Snob."

Cooper was three inches taller than Mr. Warburton, a strong, muscular young man. Mr. Warburton was fat and fifty-four. His clenched fist shot out. Cooper caught him by the arm and pushed him back.

"Don't be a damned fool. Remember I'm not a gentleman. I know how to use my hands."

He gave a sort of hoot, and, grinning all over his pale, sharp face, jumped down the verandah steps. Mr. Warburton, his heart in his anger pounding against his ribs, sank exhausted into a chair. His body tingled as though he had prickly heat. For one horrible moment he thought he was going to cry. But suddenly he was conscious that his head-boy was on the verandah and instinctively regained control of himself. The boy came forward and filled him a glass of whisky and soda. Without a word Mr. Warburton took it and drank it to the dregs.

"What do you want to say to me?" asked Mr. Warburton, trying to force a smile on to his strained lips.

"Tuan, the assistant tuan is a bad man. Abas wishes again to leave him."

"Let him wait a little. I shall write to Kuala Solor and ask that Tuan Cooper should go elsewhere."

"Tuan Cooper is not good with the Malays."

"Leave me."

The boy silently withdrew. Mr. Warburton was left alone with his thoughts. He saw the club at Kuala Solor, the men sitting round the table in the window in their flannels, when the night had driven them in from golf and tennis, drinking whiskies and gin pahits and laughing when they told the celebrated story of the Prince of Wales and himself at Marienbad. He was hot with shame and misery. A snob! They all thought him a snob. And he had always thought them very good fellows, he had always

been gentleman enough to let it make no difference
to him that they were of very second-rate position.
He hated them now. But his hatred for them was
nothing compared with his hatred for Cooper. And
if it had come to blows Cooper could have thrashed
him. Tears of mortification ran down his red, fat
face. He sat there for a couple of hours smoking
cigarette after cigarette, and he wished he were dead.

At last the boy came back and asked him if he
would dress for dinner. Of course! He always
dressed for dinner. He rose wearily from his chair
and put on his stiff shirt and the high collar. He sat
down at the prettily decorated table and was waited
on as usual by the two boys while two others waved
their great fans. Over there in the bungalow, two
hundred yards away, Cooper was eating a filthy
meal clad only in a sarong and a baju. His feet
were bare and while he ate he probably read a de-
tective story. After dinner Mr. Warburton sat
down to write a letter. The Sultan was away, but
he wrote, privately and confidentially, to his rep-
resentative. Cooper did his work very well, he
said, but the fact was that he couldn't get on with
him. They were getting dreadfully on each other's
nerves and he would look upon it as a very great
favour if Cooper could be transferred to another
post.

He despatched the letter next morning by special
messenger. The answer came a fortnight later with
the month's mail. It was a private note and ran as
follows:

My dear Warburton:—

I do not want to answer your letter officially and so I am writing you a few lines myself. Of course if you insist I will put the matter up to the Sultan, but I think you would be much wiser to drop it. I know Cooper is a rough diamond, but he is capable, and he had a pretty thin time in the war, and I think he should be given every chance. I think you are a little too much inclined to attach importance to a man's social position. You must remember that times have changed. Of course it's a very good thing for a man to be a gentleman, but it's better that he should be competent and hard-working. I think if you'll exercise a little tolerance you'll get on very well with Cooper.

Yours very sincerely

Richard Temple.

The letter dropped from Mr. Warburton's hand. It was easy to read between the lines. Dick Temple, whom he had known for twenty years, Dick Temple, who came from quite a good county family, thought him a snob and for that reason had no patience with his request. Mr. Warburton felt on a sudden discouraged with life. The world of which he was a part had passed away, and the future belonged to a meaner generation. Cooper represented it and Cooper he hated with all his heart. He stretched out his hand to fill his glass and at the gesture his head-boy stepped forward.

"I didn't know you were there."

The boy picked up the official letter. Ah, that was why he was waiting.

"Does Tuan Cooper go, Tuan?"

"No."

"There will be a misfortune."

For a moment the words conveyed nothing to his lassitude. But only for a moment. He sat up in his chair and looked at the boy. He was all attention.

"What do you mean by that?"

"Tuan Cooper is not behaving rightly with Abas."

Mr. Warburton shrugged his shoulders. How should a man like Cooper know how to treat servants? Mr. Warburton knew the type: he would be grossly familiar with them at one moment and rude and inconsiderate the next.

"Let Abas go back to his family."

"Tuan Cooper holds back his wages so that he may not run away. He has paid him nothing for three months. I tell him to be patient. But he is angry, he will not listen to reason. If the tuan continues to use him ill there will be a misfortune."

"You were right to tell me."

The fool! Did he know so little of the Malays as to think he could safely injure them? It would serve him damned well right if he got a kris in his back. A kris. Mr. Warburton's heart seemed on a sudden to miss a beat. He had only to let things take their course and one fine day he would be rid of Cooper. He smiled faintly as the phrase, a masterly inactivity, crossed his mind. And now his heart beat a little quicker, for he saw the man he hated lying on his face in a pathway of the jungle with a knife in his back. A fit end for the cad and the bully. Mr. Warburton sighed. It was his duty to warn him and of course he must do it. He wrote a brief and formal note to Cooper asking him to come to the Fort at once.

In ten minutes Cooper stood before him. They had not spoken to one another since the day when Mr. Warburton had nearly struck him. He did not now ask him to sit down.

"Did you wish to see me?" Cooper asked.

He was untidy and none too clean. His face and hands were covered with little red blotches where mosquitoes had bitten him and he had scratched himself till the blood came. His long, thin face bore a sullen look.

"I understand that you are again having trouble with your servants. Abas, my head-boy's nephew, complains that you have held back his wages for three months. I consider it a most arbitrary proceeding. The lad wishes to leave you, and I certainly do not blame him. I must insist on your paying what is due to him."

"I don't choose that he should leave me. I am holding back his wages as a pledge of his good behaviour."

"You do not know the Malay character. The Malays are very sensitive to injury and ridicule. They are passionate and revengeful. It is my duty to warn you that if you drive this boy beyond a certain point you run a great risk."

Cooper gave a contemptuous chuckle.

"What do you think he'll do?"

"I think he'll kill you."

"Why should you mind?"

"Oh, I wouldn't," replied Mr. Warburton, with a faint laugh. "I should bear it with the utmost fortitude. But I feel the official obligation to give you a proper warning."

"Do you think I'm afraid of a damned nigger?"

"It's a matter of entire indifference to me."

"Well, let me tell you this, I know how to take care of myself; that boy Abas is a dirty, thieving rascal, and if he tries any monkey tricks on me, by God, I'll wring his bloody neck."

"That was all I wished to say to you," said Mr. Warburton. "Good evening."

Mr. Warburton gave him a little nod of dismissal. Cooper flushed, did not for a moment know what to say or do, turned on his heel and stumbled out of the room. Mr. Warburton watched him go with an icy smile on his lips. He had done his duty. But what would he have thought had he known that when Cooper got back to his bungalow, so silent and cheerless, he threw himself down on his bed and in his bitter loneliness on a sudden lost all control of himself? Painful sobs tore his chest and heavy tears rolled down his thin cheeks.

After this Mr. Warburton seldom saw Cooper, and never spoke to him. He read his Times every morning, did his work at the office, took his exercise, dressed for dinner, dined and sat by the river smoking his cheroot. If by chance he ran across Cooper he cut him dead. Each, though never for a moment unconscious of the propinquity, acted as though the other did not exist. Time did nothing to assuage their animosity. They watched one another's actions and each knew what the other did. Though Mr. Warburton had been a keen shot in his youth, with age he had acquired a distaste for killing the wild things of the jungle, but on Sundays and holidays Cooper went out with his gun: if he got something it was a triumph over Mr. Warburton; if not, Mr. Warburton shrugged his shoulders and chuckled. These counter-jumpers trying to be sportsmen! Christmas was a bad time for both of them: they ate their dinners alone, each in his own quarters, and they got deliberately drunk. They were the only white men within two hundred miles and they lived within shouting distance of each other. At the beginning of the year Cooper went down with fever, and when Mr. Warburton caught sight of him again he was surprised to see how thin he had grown. He looked ill and worn. The solitude, so much more unnatural because it was due to no necessity, was getting on his nerves. It was getting on Mr. Warburton's too, and often he could not sleep at night. He lay awake brooding. Cooper was drinking heavily and surely the breaking point was near; but in his dealings with the natives he took care to do nothing that might expose him to his chief's rebuke. They fought a grim and silent battle with one another. It was a test of endurance. The months passed, and neither gave sign of weakening. They were like men dwelling in regions of eternal night, and their souls were oppressed with the knowledge that never would the day dawn for them. It looked as though their lives

would continue for ever in this dull and hideous
monotony of hatred.

And when at last the inevitable happened it came
upon Mr. Warburton with all the shock of the unexpected. Cooper accused the boy Abas of stealing
some of his clothes, and when the boy denied the
theft took him by the scruff of the neck and kicked
him down the steps of the bungalow. The boy demanded his wages, and Cooper flung at his head
every word of abuse he knew. If he saw him in the
compound in an hour he would hand him over to
the police. Next morning the boy waylaid him outside the Fort when he was walking over to his office,
and again demanded his wages. Cooper struck him
in the face with his clenched fist. The boy fell to
the ground and got up with blood streaming from
his nose.

Cooper walked on and set about his work. But
he could not attend to it. The blow had calmed his
irritation, and he knew that he had gone too far.
He was worried. He felt ill, miserable and discouraged. In the adjoining office sat Mr. Warburton, and his impulse was to go and tell him what
he had done; he made a movement in his chair, but
he knew with what icy scorn he would listen to the
story. He could see his patronising smile. For a
moment he had an uneasy fear of what Abas might
do. Warburton had warned him all right. He
sighed. What a fool he had been! But he shrugged
his shoulders impatiently. He did not care; a fat
lot he had to live for. It was all Warburton's fault;
if he hadn't put his back up nothing like this would

have happened. Warburton had made life a hell
for him from the start. The snob. But they were
all like that: it was because he was a Colonial. It
was a damned shame that he had never got his commission in the war; he was as good as any one else.
They were a lot of dirty snobs. He was damned
if he was going to knuckle under now. Of course
Warburton would hear of what had happened; the
old devil knew everything. He wasn't afraid. He
wasn't afraid of any Malay in Borneo, and Warburton could go to blazes.

He was right in thinking that Mr. Warburton
would know what had happened. His head-boy told
him when he went in to tiffin.

"Where is your nephew now?"

"I do not know, Tuan. He has gone."

Mr. Warburton remained silent. After luncheon
as a rule he slept a little, but to-day he found himself
very wide awake. His eyes involuntarily sought the
bungalow where Cooper was now resting.

The idiot! Hesitation for a little was in Mr.
Warburton's mind. Did the man know in what peril
he was? He supposed he ought to send for him.
But each time he had tried to reason with Cooper,
Cooper had insulted him. Anger, furious anger
welled up suddenly in Mr. Warburton's heart, so
that the veins on his temples stood out and he
clenched his fists. The cad had had his warning.
Now let him take what was coming to him. It was
no business of his and if anything happened it was
not his fault. But perhaps they would wish in Kuala

Solor that they had taken his advice and transferred Cooper to another station.

He was strangely restless that night. After dinner he walked up and down the verandah. When the boy went away to his own quarters, Mr. Warburton asked him whether anything had been seen of Abas.

"No, Tuan, I think maybe he has gone to the village of his mother's brother."

Mr. Warburton gave him a sharp glance, but the boy was looking down and their eyes did not meet. Mr. Warburton went down to the river and sat in his arbour. But peace was denied him. The river flowed ominously silent. It was like a great serpent gliding with sluggish movement towards the sea. And the trees of the jungle over the water were heavy with a breathless menace. No bird sang. No breeze ruffled the leaves of the cassias. All around him it seemed as though something waited.

He walked across the garden to the road. He had Cooper's bungalow in full view from there. There was a light in his sitting-room and across the road floated the sound of rag-time. Cooper was playing his gramophone. Mr. Warburton shuddered; he had never got over his instinctive dislike of that instrument. But for that he would have gone over and spoken to Cooper. He turned and went back to his own house. He read late into the night, and at last he slept. But he did not sleep very long, he had terrible dreams, and he seemed to be awakened by a cry. Of course that was a dream too, for no cry—from the bungalow for instance—could be heard in his room. He lay awake till dawn. Then he heard hurried steps and the sound of voices, his head-boy burst suddenly into the room without his fez, and Mr. Warburton's heart stood still.

"Tuan, Tuan."

Mr. Warburton jumped out of bed.

"I'll come at once."

He put on his slippers, and in his sarong and pyjama-jacket walked across his compound and into Cooper's. Cooper was lying in bed, with his mouth open, and a kris sticking in his heart. He had been killed in his sleep. Mr. Warburton started, but not because he had not expected to see just such a sight, he started because he felt in himself a sudden glow of exultation. A great burden had been lifted from his shoulders.

Cooper was quite cold. Mr. Warburton took the kris out of the wound, it had been thrust in with such force that he had to use an effort to get it out, and looked at it. He recognised it. It was a kris that a dealer had offered him some weeks before and which he knew Cooper had bought.

"Where is Abas?" he asked sternly.

"Abas is at the village of his mother's brother."

The sergeant of the native police was standing at the foot of the bed.

"Take two men and go to the village and arrest him."

Mr. Warburton did what was immediately necessary. With set face he gave orders. His words

were short and peremptory. Then he went back to
the Fort. He shaved and had his bath, dressed and
went into the dining-room. By the side of his plate
The Times in its wrapper lay waiting for him. He
helped himself to some fruit. The head-boy poured
out his tea while the second handed him a dish of
eggs. Mr. Warburton ate with a good appetite.
The head-boy waited.

"What is it?" asked Mr. Warburton.

"Tuan, Abas, my nephew, was in the house of his
mother's brother all night. It can be proved. His
uncle will swear that he did not leave the kampong."

Mr. Warburton turned upon him with a frown.

"Tuan Cooper was killed by Abas. You know it
as well as I know it. Justice must be done."

"Tuan, you would not hang him?"

Mr. Warburton hesitated an instant, and though
his voice remained set and stern a change came into
his eyes. It was a flicker which the Malay was
quick to notice and across his own eyes flashed an
answering look of understanding.

"The provocation was very great. Abas will be
sentenced to a term of imprisonment." There was
a pause while Mr. Warburton helped himself to
marmalade. "When he has served a part of his
sentence in prison I will take him into this house
as a boy. You can train him in his duties. I have no
doubt that in the house of Tuan Cooper he got
into bad habits."

"Shall Abas give himself up, Tuan?"

"It would be wise of him."

The boy withdrew. Mr. Warburton took his

Times and neatly slit the wrapper. He loved to unfold the heavy, rustling pages. The morning, so fresh and cool, was delicious and for a moment his eyes wandered out over his garden with a friendly glance. A great weight had been lifted from his mind. He turned to the columns in which were announced the births, deaths, and marriages. That was what he always looked at first. A name he knew caught his attention. Lady Ormskirk had had a son at last. By George, how pleased the old dowager must be! He would write her a note of congratulation by the next mail.

Abas would make a very good house-boy.

That fool Cooper!

THE FORCE OF
CIRCUMSTANCE

THE FORCE OF CIRCUMSTANCE

SHE was sitting on the verandah waiting for her husband to come in for luncheon. The Malay boy had drawn the blinds when the morning lost its freshness, but she had partly raised one of them so that she could look at the river. Under the breathless sun of midday it had the white pallor of death. A native was paddling along in a dug-out so small that it hardly showed above the surface of the water. The colours of the day were ashy and wan. They were but the various tones of the heat. (It was like an Eastern melody, in the minor key, which exacerbates the nerves by its ambiguous monotony; and the ear awaits impatiently a resolution, but waits in vain.) The cicadas sang their grating song with a frenzied energy: it was as continual and monotonous as the rustling of a brook over the stones; but on a sudden it was drowned by the loud singing of a bird, mellifluous and rich; and for an instant, with a catch at her heart, she thought of the English blackbird.

Then she heard her husband's step on the gravel path behind the bungalow, the path that led to the court-house in which he had been working, and she rose from her chair to greet him. He ran up the short flight of steps, for the bungalow was built on piles, and at the door the boy was waiting to take his topee. He came into the room which served them as dining-room and parlour, and his eyes lit up with pleasure as he saw her.

"Hulloa, Doris. Hungry?"

"Ravenous."

"It'll only take me a minute to have a bath and then I'm ready.

"Be quick," she smiled.

He disappeared into his dressing-room and she heard him whistling cheerily while, with the carelessness with which she was always remonstrating, he tore off his clothes and flung them on the floor. He was twenty-nine, but he was still a schoolboy; he would never grow up. That was why she had fallen in love with him, perhaps, for no amount of affection could persuade her that he was good-looking. He was a little round man, with a red face like the full moon, and blue eyes. He was rather pimply. She had examined him carefully and had been forced to confess to him that he had not a single feature which she could praise. She had told him often that he wasn't her type at all.

"I never said I was a beauty," he laughed.

"I can't think what it is I see in you."

But of course she knew perfectly well. He was a gay, jolly little man, who took nothing very solemnly, and he was constantly laughing. He made her laugh too. He found life an amusing rather than a serious business, and he had a charming smile. When she was with him she felt happy and good-

.empered. And the deep affection which she saw in
those merry blue eyes of his touched her. It was
very satisfactory to be loved like that. Once, sitting
on his knees, during their honeymoon she had taken
his face in her hands and said to him:

"You're an ugly, little fat man, Guy, but you've
got charm. I can't help loving you."

A wave of emotion swept over her and her eyes
filled with tears. She saw his face contorted for a
moment with the extremity of his feeling and his
voice was a little shaky when he answered.

"It's a terrible thing for me to have married a
woman who's mentally deficient," he said.

She chuckled. It was the characteristic answer
which she would have liked him to make.

It was hard to realise that nine months ago she
had never even heard of him. She had met him at
a small place by the seaside where she was spending
a month's holiday with her mother. Doris was
secretary to a member of parliament. Guy was
home on leave. They were staying at the same hotel,
and he quickly told her all about himself. He was
born in Sembulu, where his father had served for
thirty years under the second Sultan, and on leaving
school he had entered the same service. He was
devoted to the country.

"After all, England's a foreign land to me," he
told her. "My home's Sembulu."

And now it was her home too. He asked her to
marry him at the end of the month's holiday. She
had known he was going to, and had decided to refuse him. She was her widowed mother's only child

and she could not go so far away from her, but when
the moment came she did not quite know what
happened to her, she was carried off her feet by an
unexpected emotion, and she accepted him. They
had been settled now for four months in the little
outstation of which he was in charge. She was
very happy.

She told him once that she had quite made up her
mind to refuse him.

"Are you sorry you didn't?" he asked, with a
merry smile in his twinkling blue eyes.

"I should have been a perfect fool if I had. What
a bit of luck that fate or chance or whatever it
was stepped in and took the matter entirely out of
my hands!"

Now she heard Guy clatter down the steps to the
bath-house. He was a noisy fellow and even with
bare feet he could not be quiet. But he uttered an
exclamation. He said two or three words in the
local dialect and she could not understand. Then
she heard some one speaking to him, not aloud, but
in a sibilant whisper. Really it was too bad of
people to waylay him when he was going to have his
bath. He spoke again and though his voice was low
she could hear that he was vexed. The other voice
was raised now; it was a woman's. Doris supposed
it was some one who had a complaint to make. It
was like a Malay woman to come in that surreptitious
way. But she was evidently getting very little from
Guy, for she heard him say: get out. That at all
events she understood, and then she heard him bolt
the door. There was a sound of the water he was

throwing over himself (the bathing arrangements still amused her, the bath-houses were under the bed-rooms, on the ground; you had a large tub of water and you sluiced yourself with a little tin pail) and in a couple of minutes he was back again in the dining-room. His hair was still wet. They sat down to luncheon.

"It's lucky I'm not a suspicious or a jealous per-son," she laughed. "I don't know that I should alto-gether approve of your having animated conversa-tions with ladies while you're having your bath."

His face, usually so cheerful, had borne a sullen look when he came in, but now it brightened.

"I wasn't exactly pleased to see her."

"So I judged by the tone of your voice. In fact, I thought you were rather short with the young per-son."

"Damned cheek, waylaying me like that!"

"What did she want?"

"Oh, I don't know. It's a woman from the kam-pong. She's had a row with her husband or some-thing."

"I wonder if it's the same one who was hanging about this morning."

He frowned a little.

"Was there some one hanging about?"

"Yes, I went into your dressing-room to see that everything was nice and tidy, and then I went down to the bath-house. I saw some one slink out of the door as I went down the steps and when I looked out I saw a woman standing there."

"Did you speak to her?"

"I asked her what she wanted and she said some-thing, but I couldn't understand."

"I'm not going to have all sorts of stray people prowling about here," he said. "They've got no right to come."

He smiled, but Doris, with the quick perception of a woman in love, noticed that he smiled only with his lips, not as usual with his eyes also, and wondered what it was that troubled him.

"What have you been doing this morning?" he asked.

"Oh, nothing much. I went for a little walk."

"Through the kampong?"

"Yes. I saw a man send a chained monkey up a tree to pick coconuts, which rather thrilled me."

"It's rather a lark, isn't it?"

"Oh, Guy, there were two little boys watching him who were much whiter than the others. I wondered if they were half-castes. I spoke to them, but they didn't know a word of English."

"There are two or three half-caste children in the kampong," he answered.

"Who do they belong to?"

"Their mother is one of the village girls."

"Who is their father?"

"Oh, my dear, that's the sort of question we think it a little dangerous to ask out here." He paused. "A lot of fellows have native wives, and then when they go home or marry, they pension them off and send them back to their village."

Doris was silent. The indifference with which he spoke seemed a little callous to her. There was al-

most a frown on her frank, open, pretty English
face when she replied.

"But what about the children?"

"I have no doubt they're properly provided for.
Within his means, a man generally sees that there's
enough money to have them decently educated.
They get jobs as clerks in a Government office, you
know; they're all right."

She gave him a slightly rueful smile.

"You can't expect me to think it's a very good
system."

"You mustn't be too hard," he smiled back.

"I'm not hard. But I'm thankful you never had
a Malay wife. I should have hated it. Just think if
those two little brats were yours."

The boy changed their plates. There was never
much variety in their menu. They started luncheon
with river fish, dull and insipid, so that a good deal
of tomato ketchup was needed to make it palatable,
and then went on to some kind of stew. Guy poured
Worcester Sauce over it.

"The old Sultan didn't think it was a white
woman's country," he said presently. "He rather encouraged people to—keep house with native girls.
Of course things have changed now. The country's
perfectly quiet and I suppose we know better how
to cope with the climate."

"But, Guy, the eldest of those boys wasn't more
than seven or eight and the other was about five."

"It's awfully lonely on an outstation. Why,
often one doesn't see another white man for six
months on end. A fellow comes out here when he's

only a boy." He gave her that charming smile of his which transfigured his round, plain face. "There are excuses, you know."

She always found that smile irresistible. It was his best argument. Her eyes grew once more soft and tender.

"I'm sure there are." She stretched her hand across the little table and put it on his. "I'm very lucky to have caught you so young. Honestly, it would upset me dreadfully if I were told that you had lived like that."

He took her hand and pressed it.

"Are you happy here, darling?"

"Desperately."

She looked very cool and fresh in her linen frock. The heat did not distress her. She had no more than the prettiness of youth, though her brown eyes were fine; but she had a pleasing frankness of expression, and her dark, short hair was neat and glossy. She gave you the impression of a girl of spirit and you felt sure that the member of parliament for whom she had worked had in her a very competent secretary.

"I loved the country at once," she said. "Although I'm alone so much I don't think I've ever once felt lonely."

Of course she had read novels about the Malay Archipelago and she had formed an impression of a sombre land with great ominous rivers and a silent, impenetrable jungle. When the little coasting steamer set them down at the mouth of the river, where a large boat, manned by a dozen Dyaks, was waiting to take them to the station, her breath was taken away by the beauty, friendly rather than awe-inspiring, of the scene. It had a gaiety, like the joyful singing of birds in the trees, which she had never expected. On each bank of the river were mangroves and nipa palms, and behind them the dense green of the forest. In the distance stretched blue mountains, range upon range, as far as the eye could see. She had no sense of confinement nor of gloom, but rather of openness and wide spaces where the exultant fancy could wander with delight. The green glittered in the sunshine and the sky was blithe and cheerful. The gracious land seemed to offer her a smiling welcome.

They rowed on, hugging a bank, and high over-head flew a pair of doves. A flash of colour, like a living jewel, dashed across their path. It was a king-fisher. Two monkeys, with their dangling tails, sat side by side on a branch. On the horizon, over there on the other side of the broad and turbid river, beyond the jungle, was a row of little white clouds, the only clouds in the sky, and they looked like a row of ballet-girls, dressed in white, waiting at the back of the stage, alert and merry, for the curtain to go up. Her heart was filled with joy; and now, remembering it all, her eyes rested on her husband with a grateful, assured affection.

And what fun it had been to arrange their living-room! It was very big. On the floor, when she ar-rived, was a torn and dirty matting; on the walls of unpainted wood hung (much too high up) photo-gravures of Academy pictures, Dyak shields and pa-

rangs.   The tables were covered with Dyak cloth in
sombre colours, and on them stood pieces of Brunei
brassware, much in need of cleaning, empty cigarette tins and bits of Malay silver.   There was a
rough wooden shelf with cheap editions of novels
and a number of old travel books in battered leather,
and another shelf was crowded with empty bottles.
It was a bachelor's room, untidy but stiff; and though
it amused her she found it intolerably pathetic.   It
was a dreary, comfortless life that Guy had led
there, and she threw her arms round his neck and
kissed him.

"You poor darling," she laughed.

She had deft hands and she soon made the room
habitable.   She arranged this and that, and what she
could not do with she turned out.   Her wedding
presents helped.   Now the room was friendly and
comfortable.   In glass vases were lovely orchids
and in great bowls huge masses of flowering shrubs.
She felt an inordinate pride because it was her house
(she had never in her life lived in anything but a
poky flat) and she had made it charming for him.

"Are you pleased with me?" she asked when she
had finished.

"Quite," he smiled.

The deliberate understatement was much to her
mind.   How jolly it was that they should understand each other so well!   They were both of them
shy of displaying emotion, and it was only at rare
moments that they used with one another anything
but ironic banter.

They finished luncheon and he threw himself into

a long chair to have a sleep. She went towards her room. She was a little surprised that he drew her to him as she passed and, making her bend down, kissed her lips. They were not in the habit of exchanging embraces at odd hours of the day.

"A full tummy is making you sentimental, my poor lamb," she chaffed him.

"Get out and don't let me see you again for at least two hours."

"Don't snore."

She left him. They had risen at dawn and in five minutes were fast asleep.

Doris was awakened by the sound of her husband's splashing in the bath-house. The walls of the bungalow were like a sounding-board and not a thing that one of them did escaped the other. She felt too lazy to move, but she heard the boy bring the tea things in, so she jumped up and ran down into her own bath-house. The water, not cold but cool, was deliciously refreshing. When she came into the sitting-room Guy was taking the rackets out of the press, for they played tennis in the short cool of the evening. The night fell at six.

The tennis-court was two or three hundred yards from the bungalow and after tea, anxious not to lose time, they strolled down to it.

"Oh, look," said Doris, "there's that girl that I saw this morning."

Guy turned quickly. His eyes rested for a moment on a native woman, but he did not speak.

"What a pretty sarong she's got," said Doris. "I wonder where it comes from."

They passed her. She was slight and small, with the large, dark, starry eyes of her race and a mass of raven hair. She did not stir as they went by, but stared at them strangely. Doris saw then that she was not quite so young as she had at first thought. Her features were a trifle heavy and her skin was dark, but she was very pretty. She held a small child in her arms. Doris smiled a little as she saw it, but no answering smile moved the woman's lips. Her face remained impassive. She did not look at Guy, she looked only at Doris, and he walked on as though he did not see her. Doris turned to him.

"Isn't that baby a duck?"

"I didn't notice."

She was puzzled by the look of his face. It was deathly white, and the pimples which not a little distressed her were more than commonly red.

"Did you notice her hands and feet? She might be a duchess."

"All natives have good hands and feet," he answered, but not jovially as was his wont; it was as though he forced himself to speak.

But Doris was not intrigued.

"Who is she, d'you know?"

"She's one of the girls in the kampong."

They had reached the court now. When Guy went up to the net to see that it was taut he looked back. The woman was still standing where they had passed her. Their eyes met.

"Shall I serve?" said Doris.

"Yes, you've got the balls on your side."

He played very badly. Generally he gave her fif-

teen and beat her, but to-day she won easily.   And
he played silently.   Generally he was a noisy player,
shouting all the time, cursing his foolishness when
he missed a ball and chaffing her when he placed one
out of her reach.

"You're off your game, young man," she cried.

"Not a bit," he said.

He began to slam the balls, trying to beat her, and
sent one after the other into the net.   She had
never seen him with that set face.   Was it possible
that he was a little out of temper because he was not
playing well?   The light fell, and they ceased to
play.   The woman whom they had passed stood in
exactly the same position as when they came and
once more, with expressionless face, she watched
them go.

The blinds on the verandah were raised now and
on the table between their two long chairs were bottles and soda-water.   This was the hour at which
they had the first drink of the day and Guy mixed a
couple of gin slings.   The river stretched widely before them and on the further bank the jungle was
wrapped in the mystery of the approaching night.   A
native was silently rowing up-stream, standing at the
bow of the boat, with two oars.

"I played like a fool," said Guy, breaking a silence.   "I'm feeling a bit under the weather."

"I'm sorry.   You're not going to have fever, are
you?"

"Oh, no.   I shall be all right to-morrow."

Darkness closed in upon them.   The frogs croaked
loudly and now and then they heard a few short

notes from some singing bird of the night. Fireflies flitted across the verandah and they made the trees that surrounded it look like Christmas trees lit with tiny candles. They sparkled softly. Doris thought she heard a little sigh. It vaguely disturbed her. Guy was always so full of gaiety.

"What is it, old man?" she said gently. "Tell mother."

"Nothing. Time for another drink," he answered breezily.

Next day he was as cheerful as ever and the mail came. The coasting steamer passed the mouth of the river twice a month, once on its way to the coalfields and once on its way back. On the outward journey it brought mail, which Guy sent a boat down to fetch. Its arrival was the excitement of their uneventful lives. For the first day or two they skimmed rapidly all that had come, letters, English papers and papers from Singapore, magazines and books, leaving for the ensuing weeks a more exact perusal. They snatched the illustrated papers from one another. If Doris had not been so absorbed she might have noticed that there was a change in Guy. She would have found it hard to describe and harder still to explain. There was in his eyes a sort of watchfulness and in his mouth a slight droop of anxiety.

Then, perhaps a week later, one morning when she was sitting in the shaded room studying a Malay grammar (for she was industriously learning the language, she heard a commotion in the compound. She heard the house-boy's voice, he was speaking angrily, the voice of another man, perhaps it was the water-carrier's, and then a woman's, shrill and vituperative. There was a scuffle. She went to the window and opened the shutters. The water-carrier had hold of a woman's arm and was dragging her along, while the house-boy was pushing her from behind with both hands. Doris recognised her at once as the woman she had seen one morning loitering in the compound and later in the day outside the tennis-court. She was holding a baby against her breast. All three were shouting angrily.

"Stop," cried Doris. "What are you doing?"

At the sound of her voice the water-carrier let go suddenly and the woman, still pushed from behind, fell to the ground. There was a sudden silence and the house-boy looked sullenly into space. The water-carrier hesitated a moment and then slunk away. The woman raised herself slowly to her feet, arranged the baby on her arm, and stood impassive, staring at Doris. The boy said something to her which Doris could not have heard even if she had understood; the woman by no change of face showed that his words meant anything to her; but she slowly strolled away. The boy followed her to the gate of the compound. Doris called to him as he walked back, but he pretended not to hear. She was growing angry now and she called more sharply.

"Come here at once," she cried.

Sullenly, avoiding her wrathful glance, he came towards the bungalow. He came in and stood at the door. He looked at her sulkily.

"What were you doing with that woman?" she asked abruptly.

"Tuan say she no come here."

"You mustn't treat a woman like that. I won't have it. I shall tell the tuan exactly what I saw."

The boy did not answer. He looked away, but she felt that he was watching her through his long eyelashes. She dismissed him.

"That'll do."

Without a word he turned and went back to the servants' quarters. She was exasperated and she found it impossible to give her attention once more to the Malay exercises. In a little while the boy came in to lay the cloth for luncheon. On a sudden he went to the door.

"What is it?" she asked.

"Tuan just coming."

He went out to take Guy's hat from him. His quick ears had caught the footsteps before they were audible to her. Guy did not as usual come up the steps immediately; he paused, and Doris at once surmised that the boy had gone down to meet him in order to tell him of the morning's incident. She shrugged her shoulders. The boy evidently wanted to get his story in first. But she was astonished when Guy came in. His face was ashy.

"Guy, what on earth's the matter?"

He flushed a sudden hot red.

"Nothing. Why?"

She was so taken aback that she let him pass into his room without a word of what she had meant to speak of at once. It took him longer than usual to have his bath and change his clothes, and luncheon was served when he came in.

"Guy," she said, as they sat down, "that woman we saw the other day was here again this morning."

"So I've heard," he answered.

"The boys were treating her brutally. I had to stop them. You must really speak to them about it."

Though the Malay understood every word she said, he made no sign that he heard. He handed her the toast.

"She's been told not to come here. I gave instructions that if she showed herself again she was to be turned out."

"Were they obliged to be so rough?"

"She refused to go. I don't think they were any rougher than they could help."

"It was horrible to see a woman treated like that. She had a baby in her arms."

"Hardly a baby. It's three years old."

"How d'you know?"

"I know all about her. She hasn't the least right to come here pestering everybody."

"What does she want?"

"She wants to do exactly what she did. She wants to make a disturbance."

For a little while Doris did not speak. She was surprised at her husband's tone. He spoke tersely. He spoke as though all this were no concern of hers. She thought him a little unkind. He was nervous and irritable.

"I doubt if we shall be able to play tennis this

afternoon," he said. "It looks to me as though we were going to have a storm."

The rain was falling when she awoke and it was impossible to go out. During tea Guy was silent and abstracted. She got her sewing and began to work. Guy sat down to read such of the English papers as he had not yet gone through from cover to cover; but he was restless; he walked up and down the large room and then went out on the verandah. He looked at the steady rain. What was he thinking of? Doris was vaguely uneasy.

It was not till after dinner that he spoke. During the simple meal he had exerted himself to be his usual gay self, but the exertion was apparent. The rain had ceased and the night was starry. They sat on the verandah. In order not to attract insects they had put out the lamp in the sitting-room. At their feet, with a mighty, formidable sluggishness, silent, mysterious and fatal, flowed the river. It had the terrible deliberation and the relentlessness of destiny.

"Doris, I've got something to say to you," he said suddenly.

His voice was very strange. Was it her fancy that he had difficulty in keeping it quite steady? She felt a little pang in her heart because he was in distress, and she put her hand gently into his. He drew it away.

"It's rather a long story. I'm afraid it's not a very nice one and I find it rather difficult to tell. I'm going to ask you not to interrupt me, or to say anything, till I've finished."

In the darkness she could not see his face, but she felt that it was haggard. She did not answer. He spoke in a voice so low that it hardly broke the silence of the night.

"I was only eighteen when I came out here. I came straight from school. I spent three months in Kuala Solor, and then I was sent to a station up the Sembulu River. Of course there was a Resident there and his wife. I lived in the court-house, but I used to have my meals with them and spend the evening with them. I had an awfully good time. Then the fellow who was here fell ill and had to go home. We were short of men on account of the war and I was put in charge of this place. Of course I was very young, but I spoke the language like a native, and they remembered my father. I was as pleased as Punch to be on my own."

He was silent while he knocked the ashes out of his pipe and refilled it. When he lit a match Doris, without looking at him, noticed that his hand was unsteady.

"I'd never been alone before. Of course at home there'd been father and mother and generally an assistant. And then at school naturally there were always fellows about. On the way out, on the boat, there were people all the time, and at K.S., and the same at my first post. The people there were almost like my own people. I seemed always to live in a crowd. I like people. I'm a noisy blighter. I like to have a good time. All sorts of things make me laugh and you must have somebody to laugh with. But it was different here. Of course it was all right in the daytime; I had my work and I could talk to the Dyaks. Although they were head-hunters in those days and now and then I had a bit of trouble with them, they were an awfully decent lot of fellows. I got on very well with them. Of course I should have liked a white man to gas to, but they were better than nothing, and it was easier for me because they didn't look upon me quite as a stranger. I liked the work too. It was rather lonely in the evening to sit on the verandah and drink a gin and bitters by myself, but I could read. And the boys were about. My own boy was called Abdul. He'd known my father. When I got tired of reading I could give him a shout and have a bit of a jaw with him.

"It was the nights that did for me. After dinner the boys shut up and went away to sleep in the kampong. I was all alone. There wasn't a sound in the bungalow except now and then the croak of the chik-chak. It used to come out of the silence, suddenly, so that it made me jump. Over in the kampong I heard the sound of a gong or fire-crackers. They were having a good time, they weren't so far away, but I had to stay where I was. I was tired of reading. I couldn't have been more of a prisoner if I'd been in jail. Night after night it was the same. I tried drinking three or four whiskies, but it's poor fun drinking alone, and it didn't cheer me up; it only made me feel rather rotten next day. I tried going to bed immediately after dinner, but I couldn't sleep. I used to lie in bed, getting hotter and hotter, and more wide awake, till I didn't know what to do with myself. By George, those nights were long.

D'you know, I got so low, I was so sorry for myself that sometimes—it makes me laugh now when I think of it, but I was only nineteen and a half—sometimes I used to cry.

"Then, one evening, after dinner, Abdul had cleared away and was just going off, when he gave a little cough. He said, wasn't I lonely in the house all night by myself? 'Oh, no, that's all right,' I said. I didn't want him to know what a damned fool I was, but I expect he knew all right. He stood there without speaking, and I knew he wanted to say something to me. 'What is it?' I said. 'Spit it out.' Then he said that if I'd like to have a girl to come and live with me he knew one who was willing. She was a very good girl and he could recommend her. She'd be no trouble and it would be some one to have about the bungalow. She'd mend my things for me. . . . I felt awfully low. It had been raining all day and I hadn't been able to get any exercise. I knew I shouldn't go to sleep for hours. It wouldn't cost me very much money, he said, her people were poor and they'd be quite satisfied with a small present. Two hundred Straits dollars. 'You look,' he said. 'If you don't like her you send her away.' I asked him where she was. 'She's here,' he said. 'I call her.' He went to the door. She'd been waiting on the steps with her mother. They came in and sat down on the floor. I gave them some sweets. She was shy, of course, but cool enough, and when I said something to her she gave me a smile. She was very young, hardly more than a child, they said she was fifteen. She was awfully pretty, and she had her best clothes on. We began to talk. She didn't say much, but she laughed a lot when I chaffed her. Abdul said I'd find she had plenty to say for herself when she got to know me. He told her to come and sit by me. She giggled and refused, but her mother told her to come, and I made room for her on the chair. She blushed and laughed, but she came, and then she snuggled up to me. The boy laughed too. 'You see, she's taken to you already,' he said. 'Do you want her to stay?' he asked. 'Do you want to?' I said to her. She hid her face, laughing, on my shoulder. She was very soft and small. 'Very well,' I said, 'let her stay.'

Guy leaned forward and helped himself to a whisky and soda.

"May I speak now?" asked Doris.

"Wait a minute, I haven't finished yet. I wasn't in love with her, not even at the beginning. I only took her so as to have somebody about the bungalow. I think I should have gone mad if I hadn't, or else taken to drink. I was at the end of my tether. I was too young to be quite alone. I was never in love with any one but you." He hesitated a moment. "She lived here till I went home last year on leave. It's the woman you've seen hanging about."

"Yes, I guessed that. She had a baby in her arms. Is that your child?"

"Yes. It's a little girl."

"Is it the only one?"

"You saw the two small boys the other day in the kampong. You mentioned them."

"She has three children then?"

"Yes."

"It's quite a family you've got."

She felt the sudden gesture which her remark forced from him, but he did not speak.

"Didn't she know that you were married till you suddenly turned up here with a wife?" asked Doris.

"She knew I was going to be married."

"When?"

"I sent her back to the village before I left here. I told her it was all over. I gave her what I'd promised. She always knew it was only a temporary arrangement. I was fed up with it. I told her I was going to marry a white woman."

"But you hadn't even seen me then."

"No, I know. But I'd made up my mind to marry when I was home." He chuckled in his old manner. "I don't mind telling you that I was getting rather despondent about it when I met you. I fell in love with you at first sight and then I knew it was either you or nobody."

"Why didn't you tell me? Don't you think it would have been only fair to give me a chance of judging for myself? It might have occurred to you that it would be rather a shock to a girl to find out that her husband had lived for ten years with another girl and had three children."

"I couldn't expect you to understand. The circumstances out here are peculiar. It's the regular thing. Five men out of six do it. I thought perhaps it would shock you and I didn't want to lose you. You see, I was most awfully in love with you. I am now, darling. There was no reason that you should ever know. I didn't expect to come back here. One seldom goes back to the same station after home leave. When we came here I offered her money if she'd go to some other village. First she said she would and then she changed her mind.

"Why have you told me now?"

"She's been making the most awful scenes. I don't know how she found out that you knew nothing about it. As soon as she did she began to blackmail me. I've had to give her an awful lot of money. I gave orders that she wasn't to be allowed in the compound. This morning she made that scene just to attract your attention. She wanted to frighten me. I couldn't go on like that. I thought the only thing was to make a clean breast of it."

There was a long silence as he finished. At last he put his hand on hers.

"You do understand, Doris, don't you? I know I've been to blame."

She did not move her hand. He felt it cold beneath his.

"Is she jealous?"

"I daresay there were all sorts of perks when she was living here, and I don't suppose she much likes not getting them any longer. But she was never in love with me any more than I was in love with her. Native women never do really care for white men, you know."

"And the children?"

"Oh, the children are all right. I've provided for them. As soon as the boys are old enough I shall send them to school at Singapore."

"Do they mean nothing to you at all?"

He hesitated.

"I want to be quite frank with you. I should be sorry if anything happened to them. When the first one was expected I thought I'd be much fonder of it than I ever had been of its mother. I suppose I should have been if it had been white. Of course, when it was a baby it was rather funny and touching, but I had no particular feeling that it was mine. I think that's what it is; you see, I have no sense of their belonging to me. I've reproached myself sometimes, because it seemed rather unnatural, but the honest truth is that they're no more to me than if they were somebody else's children. Of course a lot of slush is talked about children by people who haven't got any."

Now she had heard everything. He waited for her to speak, but she said nothing. She sat motionless.

"Is there anything more you want to ask me, Doris?" he said at last.

"No, I've got rather a headache. I think I shall go to bed." Her voice was as steady as ever. "I don't quite know what to say. Of course it's been all very unexpected. You must give me a little time to think."

"Are you very angry with me?"

"No. Not at all. Only—only I must be left to myself for a while. Don't move. I'm going to bed."

She rose from her long chair and put her hand on his shoulder.

"It's so very hot to-night. I wish you'd sleep in your dressing-room. Good night."

She was gone. He heard her lock the door of her bedroom.

She was pale next day and he could see that she had not slept. There was no bitterness in her manner, she talked as usual, but without ease; she spoke of this and that as though she were making conversation with a stranger. They had never had a quarrel, but it seemed to Guy that so would she talk if they had had a disagreement and the subsequent reconciliation had left her still wounded. The look in her eyes puzzled him; he seemed to read in them a strange fear. Immediately after dinner she said:

"I'm not feeling very well to-night. I think I shall go straight to bed."

"Oh, my poor darling, I'm so sorry," he cried.

"It's nothing. I shall be all right in a day or two."

"I shall come in and say good night to you later."

"No, don't do that. I shall try and get straight off to sleep."

"Well, then, kiss me before you go."

He saw that she flushed. For an instant she seemed to hesitate; then, with averted eyes, she leaned towards him. He took her in his arms and sought her lips, but she turned her face away and he kissed her cheek. She left him quickly and again he heard the key turn softly in the lock of her door. He flung himself heavily on the chair. He tried to read, but his ear was attentive to the smallest sound in his wife's room. She had said she was going to bed, but he did not hear her move. The silence in there made him unaccountably nervous. Shading the lamp with his hand he saw that there was a glimmer under her door; she had not put out her light. What on earth was she doing? He put down his book. It would not have surprised him if she had been angry and had made him a scene, or if she had cried; he could have coped with that; but her calmness frightened him. And then what was that fear which he had seen so plainly in her eyes? He thought once more over all he had said to her on the previous night. He didn't know how else he could have put it. After all, the chief point was that he'd done the same as everybody else, and it was all over long before he met her. Of course as things turned out he had been a fool, but any one could be wise after the event. He put his hand to his heart. Funny how it hurt him there!

"I suppose that's the sort of thing people mean when they say they're heart-broken," he said to himself. "I wonder how long it's going on like this?"

Should he knock at the door and tell her he must speak to her? It was better to have it out. He *must* make her understand. But the silence scared him. Not a sound! Perhaps it was better to leave her alone. Of course it had been a shock. He must give her as long as she wanted. After all, she knew how devotedly he loved her. Patience, that was the only thing; perhaps she was fighting it out with herself; he must give her time; he must have patience.

Next morning he asked her if she had slept better.

"Yes, much," she said.

"Are you very angry with me?" he asked piteously.

She looked at him with candid, open eyes.

"Not a bit."

"Oh, my dear, I'm so glad. I've been a brute and a beast. I know it's been hateful for you. But do forgive me. I've been so miserable."

"I do forgive you. I don't even blame you."

He gave her a little rueful smile, and there was in his eyes the look of a whipped dog.

"I haven't much liked sleeping by myself the last two nights."

She glanced away. Her face grew a trifle paler.

"I've had the bed in my room taken away. It took up so much space. I've had a little camp bed put there instead."

"My dear, what are you talking about?"

Now she looked at him steadily.

"I'm not going to live with you as your wife again."

"Never?"

She shook her head. He looked at her in a puzzled way. He could hardly believe he had heard aright and his heart began to beat painfully.

"But that's awfully unfair to me, Doris."

"Don't you think it was a little unfair to me to bring me out here in the circumstances?"

"But you just said you didn't blame me."

"That's quite true. But the other's different. I can't do it."

"But how are we going to live together like that?"

She stared at the floor. She seemed to ponder deeply.

"When you wanted to kiss me on the lips last night I—it almost made me sick."

"Doris."

She looked at him suddenly and her eyes were cold and hostile.

"That bed I slept on, is that the bed in which she had her children?" She saw him flush deeply. "Oh, it's horrible. How could you?" She wrung her hands, and her twisting, tortured fingers looked like little writhing snakes. But she made a great effort and controlled herself. "My mind is quite made up. I don't want to be unkind to you, but there are some things that you can't ask me to do. I've thought it all over. I've been thinking of nothing else since you told me, night and day, till I'm exhausted. My first instinct was to get up and go. At once. The steamer will be here in two or three days."

"Doesn't it mean anything to you that I love you?"

"Oh, I know you love me. I'm not going to do that. I want to give us both a chance. I have loved you so, Guy." Her voice broke, but she did not cry. "I don't want to be unreasonable. Heaven knows, I don't want to be unkind. Guy, will you give me time?"

"I don't know quite what you mean."

"I just want you to leave me alone. I'm frightened by the feelings that I have."

He had been right then; she was afraid.

"What feelings?"

"Please don't ask me. I don't want to say any-

thing to wound you. Perhaps I shall get over them.
Heaven knows, I want to. I'll try, I promise you.
I'll try. Give me six months. I'll do everything in
the world for you, but just that one thing." She
made a little gesture of appeal. "There's no reason
why we shouldn't be happy enough together. If you
really love me you'll—you'll have patience."

He sighed deeply.

"Very well," he said. "Naturally I don't want to
force you to do anything you don't like. It shall be
as you say."

He sat heavily for a little, as though, on a sudden
grown old, it was an effort to move; then he got up.

"I'll be getting along to the office."

He took his topee and went out.

A month passed. Women conceal their feelings
better than men and a stranger visiting them would
never have guessed that Doris was in any way troubled. But in Guy the strain was obvious; his round,
good-natured face was drawn, and in his eyes was
a hungry, harassed look. He watched Doris. She
was gay and she chaffed him as she had been used to
do; they played tennis together; they chatted about
one thing and another. But it was evident that she
was merely playing a part, and at last, unable to
contain himself, he tried to speak again of his connection with the Malay woman.

"Oh, Guy, there's no object in going back on all
that," she answered breezily. "We've said all we
had to say about it and I don't blame you for anything."

"Why do you punish me then?"

"My poor boy, I don't want to punish you. It's not my fault if . . ." She shrugged her shoulders. "Human nature is very odd."

"I don't understand."

"Don't try."

The words might have been harsh, but she softened them with a pleasant, friendly smile. Every night when she went to bed she leaned over Guy and lightly kissed his cheek. Her lips only touched it. It was as though a moth had just brushed his face in its flight.

A second month passed, then a third, and suddenly the six months which had seemed so interminable were over. Guy asked himself whether she remembered. He gave a strained attention now to everything she said, to every look on her face and to every gesture of her hands. She remained impenetrable. She had asked him to give her six months; well, he had.

The coasting steamer passed the mouth of the river, dropped their mail, and went on its way. Guy busily wrote the letters which it would pick up on the return journey. Two or three days passed by. It was a Tuesday and the prahu was to start at dawn on Thursday to await the steamer. Except at meal-time when Doris exerted herself to make conversation they had not of late talked very much together; and after dinner as usual they took their books and began to read; but when the boy had finished clearing away and was gone for the night Doris put down hers.

"Guy, I have something I want to say to you," she murmured.

His heart gave a sudden thud against his ribs and he felt himself change colour.

"Oh, my dear, don't look like that, it's not so very terrible," she laughed.

But he thought her voice trembled a little.

"Well?"

"I want you to do something for me."

"My darling, I'll do anything in the world for you."

He put out his hand to take hers, but she drew it away.

"I want you to let me go home."

"You?" he cried, aghast. "When? Why?"

"I've borne it as long as I can. I'm at the end of my tether."

"How long do you want to go for? For always?"

"I don't know. I think so." She gathered determination. "Yes, for always."

"Oh, my God!"

His voice broke and she thought he was going to cry.

"Oh, Guy, don't blame me. It really is not my fault. I can't help myself."

"You asked me for six months. I accepted your terms. You can't say I've made a nuisance of myself."

"No, no."

"I've tried not to let you see what a rotten time I was having."

"I know. I'm very grateful to you. You've been

awfully kind to me. Listen, Guy, I want to tell you again that I don't blame you for a single thing you did. After all, you were only a boy, and you did no more than the others; I know what the loneliness is here. Oh, my dear, I'm so dreadfully sorry for you. I knew all that from the beginning. That's why I asked you for six months. My common sense tells me that I'm making a mountain out of a molehill. I'm unreasonable; I'm being unfair to you. But, you see, common sense has nothing to do with it; my whole soul is in revolt. When I see the woman and her children in the village I just feel my legs shaking. Everything in this house; when I think of that bed I slept in, it gives me gooseflesh. . . . You don't know what I've endured."

"I think I've persuaded her to go away. And I've applied for a transfer."

"That wouldn't help. She'd be there always. You belong to them, you don't belong to me. I think perhaps I could have stood it if there'd only been one child, but three; and the boys are quite big boys. For ten years you lived with her." And now she came out with what she had been working up to. She was desperate. "It's a physical thing, I can't help it, it's stronger than I am. I think of those thin, black arms of hers round you and it fills me with a physical nausea. I think of you holding those little black babies in your arms. Oh, it's loathsome. The touch of you is odious to me. Each night, when I've kissed you, I've had to brace myself up to it. I've had to clench my hands and force myself to touch your cheek." Now she was clasping and unclasping her fingers in a nervous agony and her voice was out of control. "I know it's I who am to blame now. I'm a silly, hysterical woman. I thought I'd get over it. I can't, and now I never shall. I've brought it all on myself; I'm willing to take the consequences; if you say I must stay here, I'll stay, but if I stay I shall die. I beseech you to let me go."

And now the tears which she had restrained so long overflowed and she wept broken-heartedly. He had never seen her cry before.

"Of course I don't want to keep you here against your will," he said hoarsely.

Exhausted, she leaned back in her chair. Her features were all twisted and awry. It was horribly painful to see the abandonment of grief on that face which was habitually so placid.

"I'm so sorry, Guy. I've broken your life, but I've broken mine too. And we might have been so happy."

"When do you want to go? On Thursday?"

"Yes."

She looked at him piteously. He buried his face in his hands. At last he looked up.

"I'm tired out," he muttered.

"May I go?"

"Yes."

For two minutes perhaps they sat there without a word. She started when the chik-chak gave its piercing, hoarse and strangely human cry. Guy rose and went out on to the verandah. He leaned against the rail and looked at the softly flowing water. He heard Doris go into her room.

Next morning, up earlier than usual, he went to her door and knocked.

"Yes?"

"I have to go up-river to-day. I shan't be back till late."

"All right."

She understood. He had arranged to be away all day in order not to be about while she was packing. It was heart-breaking work. When she had packed her clothes she looked round the sitting-room at the things that belonged to her. It seemed dreadful to take them. She left everything but the photograph of her mother. Guy did not come in till ten o'clock at night.

"I'm sorry I couldn't get back to dinner," he said. "The headman at the village I had to go to had a lot of things for me to attend to."

She saw his eyes wander about the room and notice that her mother's photograph no longer stood in its place.

"Is everything quite ready?" he asked. "I've ordered the boatman to be at the steps at dawn."

"I told the boy to wake me at five."

"I'd better give you some money." He went to his desk and wrote out a cheque. He took some notes from a drawer. "Here's some cash to take you as far as Singapore and at Singapore you'll be able to change the cheque."

"Thank you."

"Would you like me to come to the mouth of the river with you?"

"Oh, I think it would be better if we said good-bye here."

"All right. I think I shall turn in. I've had a long day and I'm dead beat."

He did not even touch her hand. He went into his room. In a few minutes she heard him throw himself on his bed. For a little while she sat looking for the last time around that room in which she had been so happy and so miserable. She sighed deeply. She got up and went into her own room. Everything was packed except the one or two things she needed for the night.

It was dark when the boy awakened them. They dressed hurriedly and when they were ready breakfast was waiting for them. Presently they heard the boat row up to the landing-stage below the bungalow, and then the servants carried down her luggage. It was a poor pretence they made at eating. The darkness thinned away and the river was ghostly. It was not yet day, but it was no longer night. In the silence the voices of the natives at the landing-stage were very clear. Guy glanced at his wife's untouched plate.

"If you've finished we might stroll down. I think you ought to be starting."

She did not answer. She rose from the table. She went into her room to see that nothing had been forgotten and then side by side with him walked down the steps. A little winding path led them to the river. At the landing-stage the native guards in their smart uniforms were lined up and they presented arms as Guy and Doris passed. The head boatman gave her his hand as she stepped into the boat. She turned and looked at Guy. She wanted desperately to say one last word of comfort, once more to ask for his forgiveness, but she seemed to be struck dumb.

He stretched out his hand.

"Well, good-bye, I hope you'll have a jolly journey."

They shook hands.

Guy nodded to the head boatman and the boat pushed off. The dawn now was creeping along the river mistily, but the night lurked still in the dark trees of the jungle. He stood at the landing-stage till the boat was lost in the shadows of the morning. With a sigh he turned away. He nodded absent-mindedly when the guard once more presented arms. But when he reached the bungalow he called the boy. He went round the room picking out everything that had belonged to Doris.

"Pack all these things up," he said. "It's no good leaving them about."

Then he sat down on the verandah and watched the day advance gradually like a bitter, an unmerited and an overwhelming sorrow. At last he looked at his watch. It was time for him to go to the office.

In the afternoon he could not sleep, his head ached miserably, so he took his gun and went for a tramp in the jungle. He shot nothing, but he walked in order to tire himself out. Towards sunset he came back and had two or three drinks, and then it was time to dress for dinner. There wasn't much use in dressing now; he might just as well be comfortable; he put on a loose native jacket and a sarong. That was what he had been accustomed to wear before Doris came. He was barefoot. He ate his dinner listlessly and the boy cleared away and went. He sat down to read The Tatler. The bungalow was very silent. He could not read and let the paper fall on his knees. He was exhausted. He could not think and his mind was strangely vacant. The chik-chak was noisy that night and its hoarse and sudden cry seemed to mock him. You could hardly believe that this reverberating sound came from so small a throat. Presently he heard a discreet cough.

"Who's there?" he cried.

There was a pause. He looked at the door. The chik-chak laughed harshly. A small boy sidled in and stood on the threshold. It was a little half-caste boy in a tattered singlet and a sarong. It was the elder of his two sons.

"What do you want?" said Guy.

The boy came forward into the room and sat down, tucking his legs away under him.

"Who told you to come here?"

"My mother sent me. She says, do you want anything?"

Guy looked at the boy intently. The boy said nothing more. He sat and waited, his eyes cast down shyly. Then Guy in deep and bitter reflection buried his face in his hands. What was the use? It was finished. Finished! He surrendered. He sat back in his chair and sighed deeply.

"Tell your mother to pack up her things and yours.   She can come back."

"When?" asked the boy impassively.

Hot tears trickled down Guy's funny, round, spotty face.

"To-night."

THE YELLOW STREAK

THE YELLOW STREAK

THE two prahus were dropping easily down-stream, one a few yards ahead of the other, and in the first sat the two white men. After seven weeks on the rivers they were glad to know that they would lodge that night in a civilised house. To Izzart, who had been in Borneo since the war, the Dyak houses and their feasts were of course an old story; but Campion, though new to the country and at first amused by the strangeness, hankered too now for chairs to sit on and a bed to sleep in. The Dyaks were hospitable, but no one could say that there was much comfort to be found in their houses, and there was a monotony in the entertainment they offered a guest which presently grew somewhat wearisome. Every evening, as the travellers reached the landing-place, the headman, bearing a flag, and the more important members of the household, came down to the river to fetch them. They were led up to the long-house—a village really under one roof, built on piles, to which access was obtained by climbing up the trunk of a tree rudely notched into steps—and to the beating of drums and gongs walked up and down the whole length of it in long procession. On both sides serried throngs of brown people sat on their haunches and stared silently as the white men passed. Clean mats were unrolled and the guests seated themselves. The headman brought a live chicken and, holding it by the legs, waved it three times over their heads, called the spirits loudly to witness and uttered an invocation. Then various persons brought eggs. Arak was drunk. A girl, a very small shy thing with the grace of a flower but with something hieratic in her immobile face, held a cup to the white man's lips till it was empty and then a great shout arose. The men began to dance, one after the other, each treading his little measure, with his shield and his parang, to the accompaniment of drum and gong. After this had gone on for some time the visitors were taken into one of the rooms that led off the long platform on which was led the common life of the household and found their supper prepared for them. The girls fed them with Chinese spoons. Then every one grew a little drunk and they all talked till the early hours of the morning.

But now their journey was done and they were on their way to the coast. They had started at dawn. The river then was very shallow and ran clear and bright over a shingly bottom; the trees leaned over it so that above there was only a strip of blue sky; but now it had broadened out, and the men were poling no longer but paddling. The trees, bamboos, wild sago like huge bunches of ostrich feathers, trees with enormous leaves and trees with feathery foliage like the acacia, coconut trees and areca palms, with their long straight white stems, the trees on the banks were immensely and violently luxuriant. Here

and there, gaunt and naked, was the bare skeleton
of a tree struck by lightning or dead of old age, and
its whiteness against all that green was vivid. Here
and there, rival kings of the forest, tall trees soared
above the common level of the jungle. Then there
were the parasites; in the fork of two branches great
tufts of lush green leaves, or flowering creepers that
covered the spreading foliage like a bride's veil;
sometimes they wound round a tall trunk, a sheath
of splendour, and threw long flowering arms from
branch to branch. There was something thrilling in
the passionate wildness of that eager growth; it had
the daring abandon of the nomad rioting in the train
of the god.

The day wore on and now the heat was no longer
so oppressive. Campion looked at the shabby silver
watch on his wrist. It could not be long now before
they reached their destination.

"What sort of a chap is Hutchinson?" he asked.

"I don't know him. I believe he's a very good
sort."

Hutchinson was the Resident in whose house they
were to spend the night and they had sent on a Dyak
in a canoe to announce their arrival.

"Well, I hope he's got some whisky. I've drunk
enough Arak to last me a lifetime."

Campion was a mining engineer whom the Sultan
on his way to England had met at Singapore and
finding him at a loose end had commissioned to go
to Sembulu and see whether he could discover any
mineral which might be profitably worked. He sent
Willis, the Resident at Kuala Solor, instructions to

afford him every facility and Willis had put him in the care of Izzart because Izzart spoke both Malay and Dyak like a native. This was the third trip they had made into the interior and now Campion was to go home with his reports. They were to catch the Sultan Ahmed which was due to pass the mouth of the river at dawn on the next day but one, and with any luck should reach Kuala Solor on the same afternoon. They were both glad to get back to it. There was tennis and golf there, and the club with its billiard tables, food which was relatively good, and the comforts of civilisation. Izzart was glad too that he would have other society than Campion's. He gave him a sidelong glance. He was a little man with a big, bald head, and though certainly fifty, strong and wiry; he had quick, shining blue eyes and a stubbly, grey moustache. He was seldom without an old briar pipe between his broken and discoloured teeth. He was neither clean nor neat, his khaki shorts were ragged and his singlet torn; he was wearing now a battered topee. He had knocked about the world since he was eighteen and had been in South Africa, in China and in Mexico. He was good company; he could tell a story well, and he was prepared to drink and drink again with any one he met. They had got on very well together, but Izzart had never felt quite at home with him. Though they joked and laughed together, got drunk together, Izzart felt that there was no intimacy between them: for all the cordiality of their relations they remained nothing but acquaintances. He was very sensitive to the impression he made on others, and behind Campion's joviality he had felt a certain coolness; those shining blue eyes had summed him up; and it vaguely irritated Izzart that Campion had formed an opinion of him, and he did not quite know what it was. He was exasperated by the possibility that this common little man did not think entirely well of him. He desired to be liked and admired. He wanted to be popular. He wished the people he met to take an inordinate fancy to him so that he could either reject them or a trifle condescendingly bestow his friendship on them. His inclination was to be familiar with all and sundry, but he was held back by the fear of a rebuff; sometimes he had been uneasily conscious that his effusiveness surprised the persons he lavished it on.

By some chance he had never met Hutchinson, though of course he knew all about him just as Hutchinson knew all about *him*, and they would have many common friends to talk of. Hutchinson had been at Winchester, and Izzart was glad that he could tell him that he had been at Harrow.

The prahu rounded a bend in the river and suddenly, standing on a slight eminence, they saw the bungalow. In a few minutes they caught sight of the landing-stage and on it, among a little group of natives, a figure in white waving to them.

Hutchinson was a tall, stout man with a red face. His appearance led you to expect that he was breezy and self-confident, so that it was not a little surprising to discover quickly that he was diffident and even a trifle shy. When he shook hands with his guests— Izzart introduced himself and then Campion—and

led them up the pathway to the bungalow, though
he was plainly anxious to be civil it was not hard to
see that he found it difficult to make conversation.
He took them out on to the verandah and here they
found on the table glasses and whisky and soda.
They made themselves comfortable on long chairs.
Izzart, conscious of Hutchinson's slight embarrassment with strangers, expanded; he was very hearty
and voluble. He began to speak of their common
acquaintances at Kuala Solor, and he managed very
soon to slip in casually the information that he had
been at Harrow.

"You were at Winchester, weren't you?" he
asked.

"Yes."

"I wonder if you knew George Parker. He was
in my regiment. He was at Winchester. I daresay
he was younger than you."

Izzart felt that it was a bond between them that
they had been at these particular schools and it
excluded Campion, who obviously had enjoyed no
such advantage. They drank two or three whiskies.
Izzart in half an hour began to call his host Hutchie.
He talked a good deal about "my regiment"
in which he had got his company during the war,
and what good fellows his brother officers were.
He mentioned two or three names which could hardly
be unknown to Hutchinson. They were not the sort
of people that Campion was likely to have come
across and he was not sorry to administer to him a
neat snub when he claimed acquaintance with some
one he spoke of.

"Billie Meadows? I knew a fellow called Billie Meadows in Sinaloa many years ago," said Campion.

"Oh, I shouldn't think it could be the same," said Izzart, with a smile. "Billie's by way of being a peer of the realm. He's the Lord Meadows who races. Don't you remember, he owned Spring Carrots?"

Dinner-time was approaching and after a wash and brush-up they drank a couple of gin pahits. They sat down. Hutchinson had not been to Kuala Solor for the best part of a year, and had not seen another white man for three months. He was anxious to make the most of his visitors. He could give them no wine, but there was plenty of whisky and after dinner he brought out a precious bottle of Benedictine. They were very gay. They laughed and talked a great deal. Izzart was getting on famously. He thought he had never liked a fellow more than Hutchinson and he pressed him to come down to Kuala Solor as soon as he could. They would have a wonderful beano. Campion was left out of the conversation by Izzart with the faintly malicious intention of putting him in his place, and by Hutchinson through shyness; and presently, after yawning a good deal, he said he would go to bed. Hutchinson showed him to his room and when he returned Izzart said to him:

"You don't want to turn in yet, do you?"

"Not on your life. Let's have another drink."

They sat and talked. They both grew a little drunk. Presently Hutchinson told Izzart that he lived with a Malay girl and had a couple of children by her. He had told them to keep out of sight while Campion was there.

"I expect she's asleep now," said Hutchinson, with a glance at the door which Izzart knew led into his room, "but I'd like you to see the kiddies in the morning."

Just then a faint wail was heard and Hutchinson, with a "Hulloa, the little devil's awake," went to the door and opened it. In a moment or two he came out of the room with a child in his arms. A woman followed him.

"He's cutting his teeth," said Hutchinson. "It makes him restless."

The woman wore a sarong and a thin white jacket and she was barefoot. She was young, with fine dark eyes, and she gave Izzart when he spoke to her a bright and pleasant smile. She sat down and lit a cigarette. She answered the civil questions Izzart put to her without embarrassment but also without effusion. Hutchinson asked her if she would have a whisky and soda, but she refused. When the two men began to talk again in English she sat on quite quietly, faintly rocking herself in her chair, and occupied with none could tell what calm thoughts.

"She's a very good girl," said Hutchinson. "She looks after the house and she's no trouble. Of course it's the only thing to do in a place like this."

"I shall never do it myself," said Izzart. "After all, one may want to get married and then it means all sorts of botherations."

"But who wants to get married? What a life for

a white woman. I wouldn't ask a white woman to live here for anything in the world."

"Of course it's a matter of taste. If I have any kiddies I'm going to see that they have a white mother."

Hutchinson looked down at the little dark-skinned child he held in his arms. He gave a faint smile.

"It's funny how you get to like them," he said. "When they're your own it doesn't seem to matter that they've got a touch of the tar-brush."

The woman gave the child a look and getting up said she would take it back to bed.

"I should think we'd better all turn in," said Hutchinson. "God knows what the time is."

Izzart went to his room and threw open the shutters which his boy Hassan, whom he was travelling with, had closed. Blowing out the candle so that it should not attract the mosquitoes, he sat down at the window and looked at the soft night. The whisky he had drunk made him feel very wide awake, and he was not inclined to go to bed. He took off his ducks, put on a sarong and lit a cheroot. His good-humour was gone. It was the sight of Hutchinson looking fondly at the half-caste child which had upset him.

"They've got no right to have them," he said to himself. "They've got no chance in the world. Ever."

He passed his hands reflectively along his bare and hairy legs. He shuddered a little. Though he had done everything he could to develop the calves, his legs were like broomsticks. He hated them. He was uneasily conscious of them all the time. They were like a native's. Of course they were the very legs for a top-boot. In his uniform he had looked very well. He was a tall, powerful man, over six feet high, and he had a neat black moustache and neat black hair. His dark eyes were fine and mobile. He was a good-looking fellow and he knew it, and he dressed well, shabbily when shabbiness was good form, and smartly when the occasion demanded. He had loved the army, and it was a bitter blow to him when, at the end of the war, he could not remain in it. His ambitions were simple. He wanted to have two thousand a year, give smart little dinners, go to parties and wear a uniform. He hankered after London.

Of course his mother lived there, and his mother cramped his style. He wondered how on earth he could produce her if ever he got engaged to the girl of good family (with a little money) whom he was looking for to make his wife. Because his father had been dead so long and during the later part of his career was stationed in the most remote of the Malay States, Izzart felt fairly sure that no one in Sembulu knew anything about her, but he lived in terror lest some one, running across her in London, should write over to tell people that she was a half-caste. She had been a beautiful creature when Izzart's father, an engineer in the Government Service, had married her; but now she was a fat old woman with grey hair who sat about all day smoking cigarettes. Izzart was twelve years old when his father died and then he could speak Malay much more flu-

ently than English. An aunt offered to pay for his
education and Mrs. Izzart accompanied her son to
England. She lived habitually in furnished apart-
ments, and her rooms with their Oriental draperies
and Malay silver were overheated and stuffy. She
was for ever in trouble with her landladies because
she would leave cigarette-ends about. Izzart hated
the way she made friends with them: she would be
shockingly familiar with them for a time, then there
would be a falling-out, and after a violent scene she
would flounce out of the house. Her only amusement
was the pictures, and to these she went every day in
the week. At home she wore an old and tawdry
dressing-gown, but when she went out she dressed
herself—but, oh, how untidily—in extravagant colours, so that it was a mortification to her dapper
son. He quarrelled with her frequently, she made
him impatient and he was ashamed of her; and yet he
felt for her a deep tenderness; it was almost a physical bond between them, something stronger than the
ordinary feeling of mother and son, so that notwithstanding the failings that exasperated him she was
the only person in the world with whom he felt entirely at home.

It was owing to his father's position and his own
knowledge of Malay, for his mother always spoke it
to him, that after the war, finding himself with nothing to do, he had managed to enter the service of the
Sultan of Sembulu. He had been a success. He
played games well, he was strong and a good ath-
lete; in the rest-house at Kuala Solor were the cups
which he had won at Harrow for running and jump-

ing, and to these he had added since others for golf and tennis. With his abundant fund of small-talk he was an asset at parties and his cheeriness made things go. He ought to have been happy and he was wretched. He wanted so much to be popular, and he had an impression, stronger than ever at this moment, that popularity escaped him. He wondered whether by any chance the men at Kuala Solor with whom he was so hail fellow well met suspected that he had native blood in him. He knew very well what to expect if they ever found out. They wouldn't say he was gay and friendly then, they would say he was damned familiar; and they would say he was inefficient and careless, as the half-castes were, and when he talked of marrying a white woman they would snigger. Oh, it was so unfair! What difference could it make, that drop of native blood in his veins, and yet because of it they would always be on the watch for the expected failure at the critical moment. Every one knew that you couldn't rely on Eurasians, sooner or later they would let you down; he knew it too, but now he asked himself whether they didn't fail because failure was expected of them. They were never given a chance, poor devils.

But a cock crew loudly. It must be very late and he was beginning to feel chilly. He got into bed. When Hassan brought him his tea next morning he had a racking headache and when he went in to breakfast he could not look at the porridge and the bacon and eggs which were set before him. Hutchinson too was feeling none too well.

"I fancy we made rather a night of it," said his host, with a smile to conceal his faint embarrassment.

"I feel like hell," said Izzart.

"I'm going to breakfast off a whisky and soda myself," added Hutchinson.

Izzart asked for nothing better, and it was with distaste that they watched Campion eat with healthy appetite a substantial meal. Campion chaffed them.

"By God, Izzart, you're looking green about the gills," he said. "I never saw such a filthy colour."

Izzart flushed. His swarthiness was always a sensitive point with him. But he forced himself to give a cheery laugh.

"You see, I had a Spanish grandmother," he answered, "and when I'm under the weather it always comes out. I remember at Harrow I fought a boy and licked him because he called me a damned half-caste."

"You are dark," said Hutchinson. "Do Malays ever ask you if you have any native blood in you?"

"Yes, damn their impudence."

A boat with their kit had started early in the morning in order to get to the mouth of the river before them and tell the skipper of the Sultan Ahmed, if by chance he arrived before he was due, that they were on their way. Campion and Izzart were to set out immediately after tiffin in order to arrive at the place where they were to spend the night before the Bore passed. A Bore is a tidal wave that, by reason of a peculiarity in the lie of the land, surges up certain rivers, and there happened to be one on the river on which they were travelling. Hutchinson had talked to them of it the night before and Campion, who had never seen such a thing, was much interested.

"This is one of the best in Borneo. It's worth looking at," said Hutchinson.

He told them how the natives, waiting the moment, rode it and were borne up the river on its crest at a breathless and terrifying speed. He had done it once himself.

"Never no more for me," he said. "I was scared out of my wits."

"I should like to try it once," said Izzart.

"It's exciting enough, but my word, when you're in a flimsy dug-out and you know that if the native doesn't get the right moment you'll be flung out in that seething torrent and you won't have a chance in a million . . . no, it's not my idea of sport."

"I've shot a good many rapids in my day," said Campion.

"Rapids be damned. You wait till you see the Bore. It's one of the most terrifying things I know. D'you know that at least a dozen natives are drowned in it in this river alone every year?"

They lounged about on the verandah most of the morning and Hutchinson showed them the court-house. Then gin pahits were served. They drank two or three. Izzart began to feel himself, and when at length tiffin was ready he found that he had an excellent appetite. Hutchinson had boasted of his Malay curry and when the steaming, succulent dishes were placed before them they all set to ravenously. Hutchinson pressed them to drink.

"You've got nothing to do but sleep. Why shouldn't you get drunk?"

He could not bear to let them go so soon, it was good after so long to have white men to talk to, and he lingered over the meal. He urged them to eat. They would have a filthy meal that night at the long-house and nothing to drink but Arak. They had better make hay while the sun shone. Campion suggested once or twice that they should start, but Hutchinson, and Izzart too, for now he was feeling very happy and comfortable, assured him there was plenty of time. Hutchinson sent for his precious bottle of Benedictine. They had made a hole in it last night; they might as well finish it before they went.

When at last he walked down with them to the river they were all very merry and none of them was quite steady on his legs. Over the middle of the boat was an attap awning and under this Hutchinson had had a mattress laid. The crew were prisoners who had been marched down from the jail to row the white men, and they wore dingy sarongs with the prison mark. They waited at their oars. Izzart and Campion shook hands with Hutchinson and threw themselves down on the mattress. The boat pushed off. The turbid river, wide and placid, glistened in the heat of that brilliant afternoon like polished brass. In the distance ahead of them they could see the bank with its tangle of green trees. They felt drowsy, but Izzart at least found a curious enjoyment in resisting for a little while the heaviness that was creeping over him, and he made up his mind that he would not let himself fall asleep till he had finished his cheroot. At last the stub began to burn his fingers and he flung it into the river.

"I'm going to have a wonderful snooze," he said.

"What about the Bore?" asked Campion.

"Oh, that's all right. We needn't worry about that."

He gave a long and noisy yawn. His limbs felt like lead. He had one moment in which he was conscious of his delicious drowsiness and then he knew nothing more. Suddenly he was awakened by Campion shaking him.

"I say, what's that?"

"What's what?"

He spoke irritably, for sleep was still heavy upon him, but with his eyes he followed Campion's gesture. He could hear nothing, but a good way off he saw two or three white-crested waves following one another. They did not look very alarming.

"Oh, I suppose that's the Bore."

"What are we going to do about it?" cried Campion.

Izzart was scarcely yet quite awake. He smiled at the concern in Campion's voice.

"Don't worry. These fellows know all about it. They know exactly what to do. We may get a bit splashed."

But while they were saying these few words the Bore came nearer, very quickly, with a roar like the roar of an angry sea, and Izzart saw that the waves were much higher than he had thought. He did not like the look of them and he tightened his belt so

that his shorts should not slip down if the boat
were upset. In a moment the waves were upon them.
It was a great wall of water that seemed to tower
over them, and it might have been ten or twelve
feet high, but you could measure it only with your
horror. It was quite plain that no boat could
weather it. The first wave dashed over them,
drenching them all, half filling the boat with water,
and then immediately another wave struck them.
The boatmen began to shout. They pulled madly
at their oars and the steersman yelled an order. But
in that surging torrent they were helpless, and it was
frightening to see how soon they lost all control
of the boat. The force of the water turned it broad-
side on and it was carried along, helter-skelter, upon
the crest of the Bore. Another great wave dashed
over them and the boat began to sink. Izzart and
Campion scrambled out of the covered place in
which they had been lying and suddenly the boat
gave way under their feet and they found themselves
struggling in the water. It surged and stormed
around them. Izzart's first impulse was to swim
for the shore, but his boy, Hassan, shouted to him to
cling to the boat. For a minute or two they all
did this.

"Are you all right?" Campion shouted to him.

"Yes, enjoying the bath," said Izzart.

He imagined that the waves would pass by as the
Bore ascended the river and in a few minutes at the
outside they would find themselves in calm water
once more. He forgot that they were being carried
along on its crest. The waves dashed over

them. They clung to the gunwale and the base of the structure which supported the attap awning. Then a larger wave caught the boat and it turned over, falling upon them so that they lost their hold; there seemed nothing but a slippery bottom to cling to and Izzart's hands slithered helplessly on the greasy surface. But the boat continued to turn and he made a desperate grab at the gunwale, only to feel it slip out of his hands as the turn went on, then he caught the framework of the awning, and still it turned, turned slowly right round and once more he sought for a hand-hold on the bottom. The boat went round and round with a horrible regularity. He thought this must be because every one was clinging to one side of it, and he tried to make the crew go round to the other. He could not make them understand. Every one was shouting and the waves beat against them with a dull and angry roar. Each time the boat rolled over on them Izzart was pushed under water, only to come up again as the gunwale and the framework of the awning gave him something to cling to. The struggle was awful. Presently he began to get terribly out of breath, and he felt his strength leaving him. He knew that he could not hold on much longer, but he did not feel frightened, for his fatigue by now was so great that he did not very much care what happened. Hassan was by his side and he told him he was growing very tired. He thought the best thing was to make a dash for the shore, it did not look more than sixty yards away, but Hassan begged him not to. Still they were being carried along amid those seething,

pounding waves. The boat went round and round
and they scrambled over it like squirrels in a cage.
Izzart swallowed a lot of water. He felt he was
very nearly done. Hassan could not help him, but
it was a comfort that he was there, for Izzart knew
that his boy, used to the water all his life, was a
powerful swimmer. Then, Izzart did not know why,
for a minute or two the boat held bottom down-
wards, so that he was able to hold on to the gunwale.
It was a precious thing to be able to get his breath.
At that moment two dug-outs, with Malays in them
riding the Bore, passed swiftly by them. They
shouted for help, but the Malays averted their faces
and went on. They saw the white men and did not
want to be concerned in any trouble that might be-
fall them. It was agonising to see them go past, callous and indifferent in their safety. But on a sudden the boat rolled round again, round and round,
slowly, and the miserable, exhausting scramble repeated itself. It took the heart out of you. But the
short respite had helped Izzart and he was able to
struggle a little longer. Then once more he found
himself so terribly out of breath that he thought his
chest would burst. His strength was all gone and he
did not know now whether he had enough to try to
swim for the shore. Suddenly he heard a cry.

"Izzart, Izzart. Help. Help."

It was Campion's voice. It was a scream of
agony. It sent a shock all through Izzart's nerves.
Campion, Campion, what did he care for Campion?
Fear seized him, a blind, animal fear, and it gave
him a new strength. He did not answer.

"Help me, quick, quick," he said to Hassan.

Hassan understood him at once. By a miracle one of the oars was floating quite close to them and he pushed it into Izzart's reach. He placed a hand under Izzart's arm and they struck away from the boat. Izzart's heart was pounding and his breath came with difficulty. He felt horribly weak. The waves beat in his face. The bank looked dreadfully far away. He did not think he could ever reach it. Suddenly the boy cried that he could touch bottom and Izzart put down his legs; but he could feel nothing; he swam a few more exhausted strokes, his eyes fixed on the bank, and then, trying again, felt his feet sink into thick mud. He was thankful. He floundered on and there was the bank within reach of his hands, black mud in which he sank to his knees; he scrambled up, desperate to get out of the cruel water, and when he came to the top he found a little flat with tall rank grass all about it. He and Hassan sank down on it and lay for a while stretched out like dead men. They were so tired that they could not move. They were covered with black mud from head to foot.

But presently Izzart's mind began to work, and a pang of anguish on a sudden shook him. Campion was drowned. It was awful. He did not know how he was going to explain the disaster when he got back to Kuala Solor. They would blame him for it; he ought to have remembered the Bore and told the steersman to make for the bank and tie up the boat when he saw it coming. It wasn't his fault, it was the steersman's, he knew the river: why in God's

name hadn't he had the sense to get into safety?
How could he have expected that it was possible to
ride that horrible torrent? Izzart's limbs shook as
he remembered the wall of seething water that
rushed down upon them. He must get the body and
take it back to Kuala Solor. He wondered whether
any of the crew were drowned too. He felt too
weak to move, but Hassan now rose and wrang the
water out of his sarong; he looked over the river
and quickly turned to Izzart.

"Tuan, a boat is coming."

The lalang grass prevented Izzart from seeing
anything.

"Shout to them," he said.

Hassan slipped out of view and made his way
along the branch of a tree that overhung the water;
he cried out and waved. Presently Izzart heard
voices. There was a rapid conversation between the
boy and the occupants of the boat and then the boy
came back.

"They saw us capsize, Tuan," he said, "and they
came as soon as the Bore passed. There's a long-
house on the other side. If you will cross the river
they will give us sarongs and food and we can sleep
there."

Izzart for a moment felt that he could not again
trust himself on the face of the treacherous water.

"What about the other tuan?" he asked.

"They do not know."

"If he's drowned they must find the body."

"Another boat has gone up-stream."

Izzart did not know what to do. He was numb.

Hassan put his arm round his shoulder and raised him to his feet. He made his way through the thick grass to the edge of the water and there he saw a dug-out with two Dyaks in it. The river now once more was calm and sluggish; the great wave had passed and no one would have dreamed that so short a while before the placid surface was like a stormy sea. The Dyaks repeated to him what they had already told the boy. Izzart could not bring himself to speak. He felt that if he said a word he would burst out crying. Hassan helped him to get in, and the Dyaks began to pull across. He fearfully wanted something to smoke, but his cigarettes and his matches, both in a hip-pocket, were soaking. The passage of the river seemed endless. The night fell and when they reached the bank the first stars were shining. He stepped ashore and one of the Dyaks took him up to the long-house. But Hassan seized the paddle he had dropped and with the other pushed out into the stream. Two or three men and some children came down to meet Izzart and he climbed to the house amid a babel of conversation. He went up the ladder and was led with greetings and excited comment to the space where the young men slept. Rattan mats were hurriedly laid to make him a couch and he sank down on them. Some one brought him a jar of Arak and he took a long drink; it was rough and fiery, burning his throat, but it warmed his heart. He slipped off his shirt and trousers and put on a dry sarong which some one lent him. By chance he caught sight of the yellow new moon lying on her back, and it gave him a keen, almost a sensual, pleasure. He could not help thinking that he might at that moment be a corpse floating up the river with the tide. The moon had never looked to him more lovely. He began to feel hungry and he asked for rice. One of the women went into a room to prepare it. He was more himself now and he began to think again of the explanations he would make at Kuala Solor. No one could really blame him because he had gone to sleep; he certainly wasn't drunk, Hutchinson would bear him out there, and how was he to suspect that the steersman would be such a damned fool? It was just rotten luck. But he couldn't think of Campion without a shudder. At last a platter of rice was brought him and he was just about to start eating when a man ran hurriedly along and came up to him.

"The tuan's come," he cried.

"What tuan?"

He jumped up. There was a commotion about the doorway and he stepped forward. Hassan was coming quickly towards him out of the darkness, and then he heard a voice.

"Izzart: Are you there?"

Campion advanced towards him.

"Well, here we are again. By God, that was a pretty near thing, wasn't it? You seem to have made yourself nice and comfortable. My heavens, I could do with a drink."

His dank clothes clung round him and he was muddy and dishevelled. But he was in excellent spirits.

"I didn't know where the hell they were bringing

me. I'd made up my mind that I should have to spend the night on the bank. I thought you were drowned."

"Here's some Arak," said Izzart.

Campion put his mouth to the jar and drank and spluttered and drank again.

"Muck, but by God it's strong." He looked at Izzart with a grin of his broken and discoloured teeth. "I say, old man, you look as though you'd be all the better for a wash."

"I'll wash later."

"All right, so will I. Tell them to get me a sarong. How did you get out?" He did not wait for an answer. "I thought I was done for. I owe my life to these two sportsmen here." He indicated with a cheery nod two of the Dyak prisoners whom Izzart vaguely recognised as having been part of their crew. "They were hanging on to that blasted boat on each side of me and somehow they cottoned on to it that I was down and out. I couldn't have lasted another minute. They made signs to me that we could risk having a shot at getting to the bank, but I didn't think I had the strength. By George, I've never been so blown in all my life. I don't know how they managed it, but somehow they got hold of the mattress we'd been lying on, and they made it into a roll. They're sportsmen, they are. I don't know why they didn't just save themselves without bothering about me. They gave it me. I thought it a damned poor life-belt, but I saw the force of the proverb about a drowning man clutching at a straw. I caught hold of the damned thing and between them somehow or other they dragged me ashore."

The danger from which he had escaped made Campion excited and voluble; but Izzart hardly listened to what he said. He heard once more, as distinctly as though the words rang now through the air, Campion's agonised cry for help, and he felt sick with terror. The blind panic raced down his nerves. Campion was talking still, but was he talking to conceal his thoughts? Izzart looked into those bright blue eyes and sought to read the sense behind the flow of words. Was there a hard glint in them or something of cynical mockery? Did he know that Izzart, leaving him to his fate, had cut and run? He flushed deeply. After all, what was there that he could have done? At such a moment it was each for himself and the devil take the hindmost. But what would they say in Kuala Solor if Campion told them that Izzart had deserted him? He ought to have stayed, he wished now with all his heart that he had, but then, then it was stronger than himself, he couldn't. Could any one blame him? No one who had seen that fierce and seething torrent. Oh, the water and the exhaustion, so that he could have cried!

"If you're as hungry as I am you'd better have a tuck in at this rice," he said.

Campion ate voraciously, but when Izzart had taken a mouthful or two he found that he had no appetite. Campion talked and talked. Izzart listened suspiciously. He felt that he must be alert and he drank more Arak. He began to feel a little drunk.

"I shall get into the devil of a row at K.S.," he said tentatively.

"I don't know why."

"I was told off to look after you. They won't think it was very clever of me to let you get nearly drowned."

"It wasn't your fault. It was the fault of the damned fool of a steersman. After all, the important thing is that we're saved. By George, I thought I was finished once. I shouted out to you. I don't know if you heard me."

"No, I didn't hear anything. There was such a devil of a row, wasn't there?"

"Perhaps you'd got away before. I don't know exactly when you did get away."

Izzart looked at him sharply. Was it his fancy that there was an odd look in Campion's eyes?

"There was such an awful confusion," he said. "I was just about down and out. My boy threw me over an oar. He gave me to understand you were all right. He told me you'd got ashore."

The oar! He ought to have given Campion the oar and told Hassan, the strong swimmer, to give *him* his help. Was it his fancy again that Campion gave him a quick and searching glance?

"I wish I could have been of more use to you," said Izzart.

"Oh, I'm sure you had enough to do to look after yourself," answered Campion.

The headman brought them cups of Arak, and they both drank a great deal. Izzart's head began to spin and he suggested that they should turn in. Beds had been prepared for them and mosquito nets fixed. They were to set out at dawn on the rest of their journey down the river. Campion's bed was next to his, and in a few minutes he heard him snoring. He had fallen asleep the moment he lay down. The young men of the long-house and the prisoners of the boat's crew went on talking late into the night. Izzart's head now was aching horribly and he could not think. When Hassan roused him as day broke it seemed to him that he had not slept at all. Their clothes had been washed and dried, but they were bedraggled objects as they walked along the narrow pathway to the river where the prahu was waiting for them. They rowed leisurely. The morning was lovely and the great stretch of placid water gleamed in the early light.

"By George, it's fine to be alive," said Campion. He was grubby and unshaved. He took long breaths and his twisted mouth was half open with a grin. You could tell that he found the air singularly good to breathe. He was delighted with the blue sky and the sunshine and the greenness of the trees. Izzart hated him. He was sure that this morning there was a difference in his manner. He did not know what to do. He had a mind to throw himself on his mercy. He had behaved like a cad, but he was sorry, he would give anything to have the chance again, but any one might have done what he did, and if Campion gave him away he was ruined. He

could never stay in Sembulu; his name would be mud
in Borneo and the Straits Settlements. If he made
his confession to Campion he could surely get Campion to promise to hold his tongue. But would he
keep his promise? He looked at him, a shifty little
man; how could he be relied on? Izzart thought of
what he had said the night before. It wasn't the
truth, of course, but who could know that? At all
events who could prove that he hadn't honestly
thought that Campion was safe? Whatever Campion said it was only his word against Izzart's;
he could laugh and shrug his shoulders and say that
Campion had lost his head and didn't know what
he was talking about. Besides, it wasn't certain
that Campion hadn't accepted his story; in that
frightful struggle for life he could be very sure of
nothing. He had a temptation to go back to the
subject, but was afraid if he did that he would
excite suspicion in Campion's mind. He *must* hold
his tongue. That was his only chance of safety.
And when they got to K.S. he would get in his story
first.

"I should be completely happy now," said Campion, "if I only had something to smoke."

"We shall be able to get some stinkers on board."

Campion gave a little laugh.

"Human beings are very unreasonable," he said.
"At the first moment I was so glad to be alive that
I thought of nothing else, but now I'm beginning to
regret the loss of my notes and my photographs and
my shaving tackle."

Izzart formulated the thought which had lurked

at the back of his mind, but which all through the night he had refused to admit into his consciousness.

"I wish to God he'd been drowned. Then I'd have been safe."

"There she is," cried Campion suddenly.

Izzart looked round. They were at the mouth of the river and there was the Sultan Ahmed waiting for them. Izzart's heart sank: he had forgotten that she had an English skipper and that he would have to be told the story of their adventure. What would Campion say? The skipper was called Bredon and Izzart had met him often at Kuala Solor. He was a little bluff man, with a black moustache, and a breezy manner.

"Hurry up," he called out to them, as they rowed up, "I've been waiting for you since dawn." But when they climbed on board his face fell. "Hulloa, what's the matter with you?"

"Give us a drink and you shall hear all about it," said Campion, with his crooked grin.

"Come along."

They sat down under the awning. On a table were glasses, a bottle of whisky and soda water. The skipper gave an order and in a few minutes they were noisily under way.

"We were caught in the Bore,' said Izzart.

He felt he must say something. His mouth was horribly dry notwithstanding the drink.

"Were you, by Jove? You're lucky not to have been drowned. What happened?"

He addressed himself to Izzart because he knew him, but it was Campion who answered. He related the whole incident, accurately, and Izzart listened with strained attention. Campion spoke in the plural when he told the early part of the story, and then, as he came to the moment when they were thrown into the water, changed to the singular. At first it was what *they* had done and now it was what happened to *him*. He left Izzart out of it. Izzart did not know whether to be relieved or alarmed. Why did he not mention him? Was it because in that mortal struggle for life he had thought of nothing but himself or—did he *know?*

"And what happened to you?" said Captain Bredon, turning to Izzart.

Izzart was about to answer when Campion spoke.

"Until I got over to the other side of the river I thought he was drowned. I don't know how he got out. I expect he hardly knows himself."

"It was touch and go," said Izzart, with a laugh.

Why had Campion said that? He caught his eye. He was sure now that there was a gleam of amusement in it. It was awful not to be certain. He was frightened. He was ashamed. He wondered if he could not so guide the conversation, either now or later, as to ask Campion whether that was the story he was going to tell in Kuala Solor. There was nothing in it to excite any one's suspicions. But if nobody else knew, Campion knew. He could have killed him.

"Well, I think you're both of you damned lucky to be alive," said the skipper.

It was but a short run to Kuala Solor, and as they steamed up the Sembulu river Izzart moodily

watched the banks. On each side were the mangroves and the nipas washed by the water, and behind, the dense green of the jungle; here and there,
among fruit trees, were Malay houses on piles.
Night fell as they docked. Goring, of the police,
came on board and shook hands with them. He was
living at the rest-house just then, and as he set
about his work of seeing the native passengers he
told them that they would find another man, Porter
by name, staying there too. They would all meet at
dinner. The boys took charge of their kit, and Campion and Izzart strolled along. They bathed and
changed and at half-past eight the four of them
assembled in the common-room for gin pahits.

"I say, what's this Bredon tells me about your
being nearly drowned?" said Goring as he came in.

Izzart felt himself flush, but before he could
answer Campion broke in, and it seemed certain to
Izzart that he spoke in order to give the story as he
chose. He felt hot with shame. Not a word was
spoken in disparagement of him, not a word was
said of him at all; he wondered if those two men
who listened, Goring and Porter, thought it strange
that he should be left out. He looked at Campion
intently as he proceeded with his narration; he told
it rather humorously; he did not disguise the danger
in which they had been, but he made a joke of it,
so that the two listeners laughed at the quandary in
which they had found themselves.

"A thing that's tickled me since," said Campion,
"is that when I got over to the other bank I was
black with mud from head to foot. I felt I really

ought to jump in the river and have a wash, but you know I felt I'd been in that damned river as much as ever I wanted, and I said to myself: No, by George, I'll go dirty. And when I got into the long-house and saw Izzart as black as I was, I knew he'd felt just like I did."

They laughed and Izzart forced himself to laugh too. He noticed that Campion had told the story in precisely the same words as he had used when he told it to the skipper of the Sultan Ahmed. There could be only one explanation of that; he knew, he knew everything, and had made up his mind exactly what story to tell. The ingenuity with which Campion gave the facts and yet left out what must be to Izzart's discredit was devilish. But why was he holding his hand? It wasn't in him not to feel contempt and resentment for the man who had callously deserted him in that moment of dreadful peril. Suddenly, in a flash of inspiration Izzart understood: he was keeping the truth to tell to Willis, the Resident. Izzart had gooseflesh as he thought of confronting Willis. He could deny, but would his denials serve him? Willis was no fool and he would get at Hassan; Hassan could not be trusted to be silent; Hassan would give him away. Then he would be done for. Willis would suggest that he had better go home.

He had a racking headache and after dinner he went to his room, for he wanted to be alone so that he could devise a plan of action. And then a thought came to him which made him go hot and cold; he knew that the secret which he had guarded so long was a secret to nobody. He was on a sudden certain of it. Why should he have those bright eyes and that swarthy skin? Why should he speak Malay with such ease and have learned Dyak so quickly? Of course they knew. What a fool he was ever to think that they believed that story of his, about the Spanish grandmother! They must have laughed up their sleeves when he told it, and behind his back they had called him a damned nigger. And now another thought came to him, torturing, and he asked himself whether it was on account of that wretched drop of native blood in him that when he heard Campion cry out his nerve failed him. After all, any one might at that moment have been seized with panic; and why in God's name should he sacrifice his life to save a man's whom he cared nothing for? It was insane. But of course in K.S. they would say it was only what they expected; they would make no allowances.

At last he went to bed, but when, after tossing about restlessly for God knows how long, he fell asleep, he was awakened by a fearful dream; he seemed to be once more in that raging torrent, with the boat turning, turning; and then there was the desperate clutching at the gunwale, and the agony as it slipped out of his hands, and the water that roared over him. He was wide awake before dawn. His only chance was to see Willis and get his story in first; and he thought over carefully what he was going to say and chose the very words he meant to use.

He got up early, and in order not to see Campion

went out without breakfast. He walked along the highroad till such time as he knew the Resident would be in his office and then walked back again. He sent in his name and was ushered into Willis's room. He was a little elderly man with thin grey hair and a long yellow face.

"I'm glad to see you back safe and sound," he said, shaking hands with Izzart. "What's this I hear about your being nearly drowned?"

Izzart, in clean ducks, his topee spotless, was a fine figure of a man. His black hair was neatly brushed and his moustache was trimmed. He had an upright and soldierly bearing.

"I thought I'd better come and tell you at once, sir, as you told me to look after Campion."

"Fire away."

Izzart told his story. He made light of the danger. He gave Willis to understand that it had not been very great. They would never have been upset if they had not started so late.

"I tried to get Campion away earlier, but he'd had two or three drinks and the fact is, he didn't want to move."

"Was he tight?"

"I don't know about that," smiled Izzart good-humouredly. "I shouldn't say he was cold sober."

He went on with his story. He managed to insinuate that Campion had lost his head a little. Of course it was a very frightening business to a man who wasn't a decent swimmer: he, Izzart, had been more concerned for Campion than for himself; he knew the only chance was to keep cool, and the moment they were upset he saw that Campion had got the wind up.

"You can't blame him for that," said the Resident.

"Of course I did everything I possibly could for him, sir, but the fact is, there wasn't anything much I could do."

"Well, the great thing is that you both escaped. It would have been very awkward for all of us if he'd been drowned."

"I thought I'd better come and tell you the facts before you saw Campion, sir. I fancy he's inclined to talk rather wildly about it. There's no use exaggerating."

"On the whole your stories agree pretty well," said Willis, with a little smile.

Izzart looked at him blankly.

"Haven't you seen Campion this morning? I heard from Goring that there'd been some trouble and I looked in last night on my way home from the Fort after dinner. You'd already gone to bed."

Izzart felt himself trembling and he made a great effort to preserve his composure.

"By the way, you got away first, didn't you?"

"I don't really know, sir. You see, there was a lot of confusion."

"You must have if you got over to the other side before he did."

"I suppose I did then."

"Well, thanks for coming to tell me," said Willis, rising from his chair.

As he did so he knocked some books on the floor. They fell with a sudden thud. The unexpected sound made Izzart start violently and he gave a gasp. The Resident looked at him quickly.

"I say, your nerves are in a pretty state."

Izzart could not control his trembling.

"I'm very sorry, sir," he murmured.

"I expect it's been a shock. You'd better take it easy for a few days. Why don't you get the doctor to give you something?"

"I didn't sleep very well last night."

The Resident nodded as though he understood. Izzart left the room, and as he passed out some man he knew stopped and congratulated him on his escape. They all knew of it. He walked back to the rest-house. And as he walked he repeated to himself the story he had told the Resident. Was it really the same story that Campion had told? He had never suspected that the Resident had already heard it from Campion. What a fool he had been to go to bed! He should never have let Campion out of his sight. Why had the Resident listened without telling him that he already knew? Now Izzart cursed himself for having suggested that Campion was drunk and had lost his head. He had said this in order to discredit him, but he knew now that it was a stupid thing to do. And why had Willis said that about his having got away first? Perhaps he was holding his hand too; perhaps he was going to make enquiries; Willis was very shrewd. But what exactly had Campion said? He must know that; at whatever cost he must know. Izzart's mind was seething so that he felt he could hardly keep a hold on his thoughts, but he must keep calm. He

felt like a hunted animal. He did not believe that
Willis liked him; once or twice in the office he had
blamed him because he was careless; perhaps he was
just waiting till he got all the facts. Izzart was
almost hysterical.

He entered the rest-house and there, sitting on a
long chair, with his legs stretched out, was Campion.
He was reading the papers which had arrived during
their absence in the jungle. Izzart felt a blind rush
of hatred well up in him as he looked at the little,
shabby man who held him in the hollow of his hand.

"Hulloa," said Campion, looking up. "Where
have you been?"

To Izzart it seemed that there was in his eyes a
mocking irony. He clenched his hands and his
breath came fast.

"What have you been saying to Willis about me?"
he asked abruptly.

The tone in which he put the unexpected question
was so harsh that Campion gave him a glance of
faint surprise.

"I don't think I've been saying anything very much
about you. Why?"

"He came here last night."

Izzart looked at him intently. His brows were
drawn together in an angry frown as he tried to
read Campion's thoughts.

"I told him you'd gone to bed with a headache.
He wanted to know about our mishap."

"I've just seen him."

Izzart walked up and down the large and shaded
room; now, though it was still early, the sun was hot

and dazzling. He felt himself in a net. He was blind with rage; he could have seized Campion by the throat and strangled him, and yet, because he did not know what he had to fight against, he felt himself powerless. He was tired and ill, and his nerves were shaken. On a sudden the anger which had given him a sort of strength left him and he was filled with despondency. It was as though water and not blood ran through his veins; his heart sank and his knees seemed to give way. He felt that if he did not take care he would begin to cry. He was dreadfully sorry for himself.

"Damn you, I wish to God I'd never set eyes on you," he cried pitifully.

"What on earth's the matter?" asked Campion, with astonishment.

"Oh, don't pretend. We've been pretending for two days and I'm fed up with it." His voice rose shrilly, it sounded odd in that robust and powerful man. "I'm fed up with it. I cut and run. I left you to drown. I know I behaved like a skunk. I couldn't help it."

Campion rose slowly from his chair.

"What *are* you talking about?"

His tone was so genuinely surprised that it gave Izzart a start. A cold shiver ran down his spine.

"When you called for help I was panic-stricken. I just caught hold of an oar and got Hassan to help me get away."

"That was the most sensible thing you could do."

"I couldn't help you. There wasn't a thing I could do."

"Of course not. It was damned silly of me to shout. It was waste of breath, and breath was the very thing I wanted."

"Do you mean to say you didn't know?"

"When those fellows got me the mattress I thought you were still clinging to the boat. I had an idea that I got away before you did."

Izzart put both his hands to his head and gave a hoarse cry of despair.

"My God, what a fool I've been."

The two men stood for a while staring at one another. The silence seemed endless.

"What are you going to do now?" asked Izzart at last.

"Oh, my dear fellow, don't worry. I've been frightened too often myself to blame any one who shows the white feather. I'm not going to tell a soul."

"Yes, but you *know*."

"I promise you, you can trust me. Besides, my job's done here and I'm going home. I want to catch the next boat to Singapore." There was a pause, and Campion looked for a while reflectively at Izzart. "There's only one thing I'd like to ask you: I've made a good many friends here, and there are one or two things I'm a little sensitive about; when you tell the story of our upset I should be grateful if you wouldn't make out that I had behaved badly. I wouldn't like the fellows here to think that I'd lost my nerve."

Izzart flushed darkly. He remembered what he had said to the Resident. It almost looked as though

Campion had been listening over his shoulder. He cleared his throat.

"I don't know why you think I should do that."

Campion chuckled good-naturedly, and his blue eyes were gay with amusement.

"The yellow streak," he replied, and then, with a grin that showed his broken and discoloured teeth: "Have a cheroot, dear boy."

THE LETTER

THE LETTER

OUTSIDE on the quay the sun beat fiercely. A stream of motors, lorries and busses, private cars and hirelings, sped up and down the crowded thoroughfare, and every chauffeur blew his horn; rickshaws threaded their nimble path amid the throng, and the panting coolies found breath to yell at one another; coolies, carrying heavy bales, sidled along with their quick jog-trot and shouted to the passer-by to make way; itinerant vendors proclaimed their wares. Singapore is the meeting-place of a hundred peoples; and men of all colours, black Tamils, yellow Chinks, brown Malays, Armenians, Jews and Bengalis, called to one another in raucous tones. But inside the office of Messrs. Ripley, Joyce & Naylor it was pleasantly cool; it was dark after the dusty glitter of the street and agreeably quiet after its unceasing din. Mr. Joyce sat in his private room, at the table, with an electric fan turned full on him. He was leaning back, his elbows on the arms of the chair, with the tips of the outstretched fingers of one hand resting neatly against the tips of the outstretched fingers of the other. His gaze rested on the battered volumes of the Law Reports which stood on a long shelf in front of him. On the top of a cupboard were square boxes of japanned tin on which were painted the names of various clients.

There was a knock at the door.

"Come in."

A Chinese clerk, very neat in his white ducks, opened it.

"Mr. Crosbie is here, sir."

He spoke beautiful English, accenting each word with precision, and Mr. Joyce had often wondered at the extent of his vocabulary. Ong Chi Seng was a Cantonese, and he had studied law at Gray's Inn. He was spending a year or two with Messrs. Ripley, Joyce & Naylor in order to prepare himself for practice on his own account. He was industrious, obliging, and of exemplary character.

"Show him in," said Mr. Joyce.

He rose to shake hands with his visitor and asked him to sit down. The light fell on him as he did so. The face of Mr. Joyce remained in shadow. He was by nature a silent man, and now he looked at Robert Crosbie for quite a minute without speaking. Crosbie was a big fellow well over six feet high, with broad shoulders, and muscular. He was a rubber-planter, hard with the constant exercise of walking over the estate and with the tennis which was his relaxation when the day's work was over. He was deeply sunburned. His hairy hands, his feet in clumsy boots, were enormous, and Mr. Joyce found himself thinking that a blow of that great fist would easily kill the fragile Tamil. But there was no fierceness in his blue eyes; they were confiding and gentle; and his face, with its big, undistinguished features, was open, frank and honest. But at this moment it bore a look of deep distress. It was drawn and haggard.

"You look as though you hadn't had much sleep the last night or two," said Mr. Joyce.

"I haven't."

Mr. Joyce noticed now the old felt hat, with its broad double brim, which Crosbie had placed on the table; and then his eyes travelled to the khaki shorts he wore, showing his red hairy thighs, the tennis shirt open at the neck, without a tie, and the dirty khaki jacket with the ends of the sleeves turned up. He looked as though he had just come in from a long tramp among the rubber trees. Mr. Joyce gave a slight frown.

"You must pull yourself together, you know. You must keep your head."

"Oh, I'm all right."

"Have you seen your wife to-day?"

"No, I'm to see her this afternoon. You know, it is a damned shame that they should have arrested her."

"I think they had to do that," Mr. Joyce answered in his level, soft tone.

"I should have thought they'd have let her out on bail."

"It's a very serious charge."

"It is damnable. She did what any decent woman would do in her place. Only, nine women out of ten wouldn't have the pluck. Leslie's the best woman in the world. She wouldn't hurt a fly. Why, hang it all, man, I've been married to her for twelve

years, do you think I don't know her? God, if I'd
got hold of the man I'd have wrung his neck. I'd
have killed him without a moment's hesitation. So
would you."

"My dear fellow, everybody's on your side. No
one has a good word to say for Hammond. We're
going to get her off. I don't suppose either the
assessors or the judge will go into court without
having already made up their minds to bring in a
verdict of not guilty."

"The whole thing's a farce," said Crosbie
violently. "She ought never to have been arrested
in the first place, and then it's terrible, after all the
poor girl's gone through, to subject her to the ordeal
of a trial. There's not a soul I've met since I've
been in Singapore, man or woman, who hasn't told
me that Leslie was absolutely justified. I think it's
awful to keep her in prison all these weeks."

"The law is the law. After all, she confesses that
she killed the man. It is terrible, and I'm dreadfully sorry both for you and for her."

"I don't matter a hang," interrupted Crosbie.

"But the fact remains that murder has been committed, and in a civilised community a trial is inevitable."

"Is it murder to exterminate noxious vermin?
She shot him as she would have shot a mad dog."

Mr. Joyce leaned back again in his chair and once
more placed the tips of his ten fingers together. The
little construction he formed looked like the skeleton of a roof. He was silent for a moment.

"I should be wanting in my duty as your legal

adviser," he said at last, in an even voice, looking at his client with his cool, brown eyes, "if I did not tell you that there is one point which causes me just a little anxiety. If your wife had only shot Hammond once, the whole thing would be absolutely plain sailing. Unfortunately she fired six times."

"Her explanation is perfectly simple. In the circumstances any one would have done the same."

"I daresay," said Mr. Joyce, "and of course I think the explanation is very reasonable. But it's no good closing our eyes to the facts. It's always a good plan to put yourself in another man's place, and I can't deny that if I were prosecuting for the Crown that's the point on which I should centre my enquiry."

"My dear fellow, that's perfectly idiotic."

Mr. Joyce shot a sharp glance at Robert Crosbie. The shadow of a smile hovered over his shapely lips. Crosbie was a good fellow, but he could hardly be described as intelligent.

"I daresay it's of no importance," answered the lawyer, "I just thought it was a point worth mentioning. You haven't got very long to wait now, and when it's all over I recommend you to go off somewhere with your wife on a trip and forget all about it. Even though we are almost dead certain to get an acquittal, a trial of that sort is anxious work and you'll both want a rest."

For the first time Crosbie smiled, and his smile strangely changed his face. You forgot the uncouthness and saw only the goodness of his soul.

"I think I shall want it more than Leslie. She's

borne up wonderfully.   By God, there's a plucky little woman for you."

"Yes, I've been very much struck by her self-control," said the lawyer.   "I should never have guessed that she was capable of such determination."

His duties as her counsel had made it necessary for him to have a good many interviews with Mrs. Crosbie since her arrest. Though things had been made as easy as could be for her, the fact remained that she was in jail, awaiting her trial for murder, and it would not have been surprising if her nerves had failed her.   She appeared to bear her ordeal with composure.   She read a great deal, took such exercise as was possible, and by favour of the authorities worked at the pillow lace which had always formed the entertainment of her long hours of leisure.   When Mr. Joyce saw her she was neatly dressed in cool, fresh, simple frocks, her hair was carefully arranged, and her nails were manicured. Her manner was collected.   She was able even to jest upon the little inconveniences of her position. There was something casual about the way in which she spoke of the tragedy, which suggested to Mr. Joyce that only her good breeding prevented her from finding something a trifle ludicrous in a situation which was eminently serious.   It surprised him, for he had never thought that she had a sense of humour.

He had known her off and on for a good many years.   When she paid visits to Singapore she generally came to dine with his wife and himself, and once or twice she had passed a week-end with them at their bungalow by the sea. His wife had spent a fortnight with her on the estate and had met Geoffrey Hammond several times. The two couples had been on friendly, if not on intimate, terms, and it was on this account that Robert Crosbie had rushed over to Singapore immediately after the catastrophe and begged Mr. Joyce to take charge personally of his unhappy wife's defence.

The story she told him the first time he saw her, she had never varied in the smallest detail. She told it as coolly then, a few hours after the tragedy, as she told it now. She told it connectedly, in a level, even voice, and her only sign of confusion was when a slight colour came into her cheeks as she described one or two of its incidents. She was the last woman to whom one would have expected such a thing to happen. She was in the early thirties, a fragile creature, neither short nor tall, and graceful rather than pretty. Her wrists and ankles were very delicate, but she was extremely thin and you could see the bones of her hands through the white skin, and the veins were large and blue. Her face was colourless, slightly sallow, and her lips were pale. You did not notice the colour of her eyes. She had a great deal of light brown hair and it had a slight natural wave; it was the sort of hair that with a little touching-up would have been very pretty, but you could not imagine that Mrs. Crosbie would think of resorting to any such device. She was a quiet, pleasant, unassuming woman. Her manner was engaging and if she was not very popular it was because she suffered from a certain shyness.

This was comprehensible enough, for the planter's
life is lonely, and in her own house, with people she
knew, she was in her quiet way charming. Mrs.
Joyce after her fortnight's stay had told her husband that Leslie was a very agreeable hostess.
There was more in her, she said, than people
thought; and when you came to know her you were
surprised how much she had read and how entertain-
ing she could be.

She was the last woman in the world to commit
murder.

Mr. Joyce dismissed Robert Crosbie with such
reassuring words as he could find and, once more
alone in his office, turned over the pages of the
brief. But it was a mechanical action, for all its
details were familiar to him. The case was the sensation of the day, and it was discussed in all the
clubs, at all the dinner tables, up and down the
Peninsula from Singapore to Penang. The facts
that Mrs. Crosbie gave were simple. Her husband
had gone to Singapore on business and she was alone
for the night. She dined by herself, late, at a quarter to nine, and after dinner sat in the sitting-room
working at her lace. It opened on to the verandah.
There was no one in the bungalow, for the servants
had retired to their own quarters at the back of
the compound. She was surprised to hear a step on
the gravel path in the garden, a booted step which
suggested a white man rather than a native, for
she had not heard a motor drive up and she could
not imagine who could be coming to see her at that
time of night. Some one ascended the few stairs

that led up to the bungalow, walked across the verandah, and appeared at the door of the room in which she sat. At the first moment she did not recognise the visitor. She sat with a shaded lamp and he stood with his back to the darkness.

"May I come in?" he said.

She did not even recognise the voice.

"Who is it?" she asked.

She worked with spectacles, and she took them off as she spoke.

"Geoff. Hammond."

"Of course. Come in and have a drink."

She rose and shook hands with him cordially. She was a little surprised to see him, for though he was a neighbour neither she nor Robert had been lately on very intimate terms with him, and she had not seen him for some weeks. He was the manager of a rubber estate nearly eight miles from theirs and she wondered why he had chosen this late hour to come and see them.

"Robert's away," she said. "He had to go to Singapore for the night."

Perhaps he thought his visit called for some explanation, for he said:

"I'm sorry. I felt rather lonely to-night, so I thought I'd just come along and see how you were getting on."

"How on earth did you come? I never heard a car."

"I left it down the road. I thought you might both be in bed and asleep."

This was natural enough. The planter gets up

at dawn in order to take the roll-call of the workers, and soon after dinner he is glad to go to bed. Hammond's car was in point of fact found next day a quarter of a mile from the bungalow.

Since Robert was away there was no whisky and soda in the room. Leslie did not call the boy, since he was probably asleep, but fetched it herself. Her guest mixed himself a drink and filled his pipe.

Geoff. Hammond had a host of friends in the colony. He was at this time in the late thirties, but he had come out as a lad. He had been one of the first to volunteer on the outbreak of war, and had done very well. A wound in the knee caused him to be invalided out of the army after two years, but he returned to the Federated Malay States with a D.S.O. and an M.C. He was one of the best billiard-players in the colony. He had been a beautiful dancer and a fine tennis player, but, though able no longer to dance, and his tennis, with a stiff knee, was not so good as it had been, he had the gift of popularity and was universally liked. He was a tall, good-looking fellow, with attractive blue eyes and a fine head of black, curling hair. Old stagers said his only fault was that he was too fond of the girls, and after the catastrophe they shook their heads and vowed that they had always known this would get him into trouble.

He began now to talk to Leslie about the local affairs, the forthcoming races in Singapore, the price of rubber, and his chances of killing a tiger which had been lately seen in the neighbourhood. She was anxious to finish by a certain date, the piece of lace on which she was working, for she wanted to send it home for her mother's birthday, and so put on her spectacles again and drew towards her chair the little table on which stood the pillow.

"I wish you wouldn't wear those great horn-spectacles," he said. "I don't know why a pretty woman should do her best to look plain."

She was a trifle taken aback at this remark. He had never used that tone with her before. She thought the best thing was to make light of it.

"I have no pretensions to being a raving beauty, you know, and, if you ask me point blank, I'm bound to tell you that I don't care two pins if you think me plain or not."

"I don't think you're plain. I think you're awfully pretty."

"Sweet of you," she answered ironically. "But in that case I can only think you half-witted."

He chuckled. But he rose from his chair and sat down in another by her side.

"You're not going to have the face to deny that you have the prettiest hands in the world," he said.

He made a gesture as though to take one of them. She gave him a little tap.

"Don't be an idiot. Sit down where you were before and talk sensibly, or else I shall send you home."

He did not move.

"Don't you know that I'm awfully in love with you?" he said.

She remained quite cool.

"I don't. I don't believe it for a minute, and even if it were true I don't want you to say it."

She was the more surprised at what he was saying, since during the seven years she had known him he had never paid her any particular attention. When he came back from the war they had seen a good deal of one another, and once when he was ill Robert had gone over and brought him back to their bungalow in his car. He had stayed with them then for a fortnight. But their interests were dissimilar and the acquaintance had never ripened into friendship. For the last two or three years they had seen little of him. Now and then he came over to play tennis, now and then they met him at some planter's who was giving a party, but it often happened that they did not set eyes on him for a month at a time.

Now he took another whisky and soda. Leslie wondered if he had been drinking before. There was something odd about him, and it made her a trifle uneasy. She watched him help himself with disapproval.

"I wouldn't drink any more if I were you," she said, good-humouredly still.

He emptied his glass and put it down.

"Do you think I'm talking to you like this because I'm drunk?" he asked abruptly.

"That is the most obvious explanation, isn't it?"

"Well, it's a lie. I've loved you ever since I first knew you. I've held my tongue as long as I could, and now it's got to come out. I love you, I love you, I love you."

She rose and carefully put aside the pillow.

"Good night," she said.

"I'm not going now."

At last she began to lose her temper.

"But, you poor fool, don't you know that I've never loved any one but Robert, and even if I didn't love Robert you're the last man I should care for."

"What do I care? Robert's away."

"If you don't go away this minute I shall call the boys and have you thrown out."

"They're out of earshot."

She was very angry now. She made a movement as though to go on to the verandah from which the house-boy would certainly hear her, but he seized her arm.

"Let me go," she cried furiously.

"Not much. I've got you now."

She opened her mouth and called "Boy, boy," but with a quick gesture he put his hand over it. Then before she knew what he was about he had taken her in his arms and was kissing her passionately. She struggled, turning her lips away from his burning mouth.

"No, no, no," she cried. "Leave me alone. I won't."

She grew confused about what happened then. All that had been said before she remembered accurately, but now his words assailed her ears through a mist of horror and fear. He seemed to plead for her love. He broke into violent protestations of passion. And all the time he held her in his tempestuous embrace. She was helpless, for he was a strong, powerful man, and her arms were pinioned to her sides; her struggles were unavailing and she felt herself growing weaker; she was afraid she would faint, and his hot breath on her face made her feel desperately sick. He kissed her mouth, her eyes, her cheeks, her hair. The pressure of his arms was killing her. He lifted her off her feet. She tried to kick him, but he only held her more closely. He was carrying her now. He wasn't speaking any more, but she knew that his face was pale and his eyes hot with desire. He was taking her into the bedroom. He was no longer a civilised man, but a savage. And as he ran he stumbled against a table which was in the way. His stiff knee made him a little awkward on his feet, and with the burden of the woman in his arms he fell. In a moment she had snatched herself away from him. She ran round the sofa. He was up in a flash and flung himself towards her. There was a revolver on the desk. She was not a nervous woman, but Robert was to be away for the night and she had meant to take it into her room when she went to bed. That was why it happened to be there. She was frantic with terror now. She did not know what she was doing. She heard a report. She saw Hammond stagger. He gave a cry. He said something, she didn't know what. He lurched out of the room on to the verandah. She was in a frenzy now, she was beside herself, she followed him out, yes, that was it, she must have followed him out, though she remembered nothing of it, she followed firing automatically shot after shot till the six chambers were empty. Hammond fell down on the floor of the verandah. He crumpled up into a bloody heap.

When the boys, startled by the reports, rushed up, they found her standing over Hammond with the revolver still in her hand, and Hammond lifeless. She looked at them for a moment without speaking. They stood in a frightened, huddled bunch. She let the revolver fall from her hand and without a word turned and went into the sitting-room. They watched her go into her bedroom and turn the key in the lock. They dared not touch the dead body, but looked at it with terrified eyes, talking excitedly to one another in undertones. Then the head-boy collected himself; he had been with them for many years, he was Chinese and a level-headed fellow. Robert had gone into Singapore on his motor-cycle and the car stood in the garage. He told the seis to get it out; they must go at once to the Assistant District Officer and tell him what had happened. He picked up the revolver and put it in his pocket. The A.D.O., a man called Withers, lived on the outskirts of the nearest town, which was about thirty-five miles away. It took them an hour and a half to reach him. Every one was asleep, and they had to rouse the boys. Presently Withers came out and they told him their errand. The head-boy showed him the revolver in proof of what he said. The A.D.O. went into his room to dress, sent for his car, and in a little while was following them back along the deserted road. The dawn was just breaking as he reached the Crosbies' bungalow. He ran up the steps of the verandah, and stopped short as he saw Hammond's body lying where he fell. He touched the face. It was quite cold.

"Where's mem?" he asked the house-boy.

The Chinese pointed to the bedroom. Withers went to the door and knocked. There was no answer. He knocked again.

"Mrs. Crosbie," he called.

"Who is it?"

"Withers."

There was another pause. Then the door was unlocked and slowly opened. Leslie stood before him. She had not been to bed and wore the tea-gown in which she had dined. She stood and looked silently at the A.D.O.

"Your house-boy fetched me," he said. "Hammond. What have you done?"

"He tried to rape me and I shot him."

"My God! I say, you'd better come out here. You must tell me exactly what happened."

"Not now. I can't. You must give me time. Send for my husband."

Withers was a young man, and he did not know exactly what to do in an emergency which was so out of the run of his duties. Leslie refused to say anything till at last Robert arrived. Then she told the two men the story, from which since then, though she had repeated it over and over again, she had never in the slightest degree diverged.

The point to which Mr. Joyce recurred was the shooting. As a lawyer he was bothered that Leslie had fired not once but six times, and the examination of the dead man showed that four of the shots had been fired close to the body. One might almost have thought that when the man fell she stood over him and emptied the contents of the revolver into him. She confessed that her memory, so accurate for all that had preceded, failed her here. Her mind was blank. It pointed to an uncontrollable fury; but uncontrollable fury was the last thing you would have expected from this quiet and demure woman. Mr. Joyce had known her a good many years, and had always thought her an unemotional person; during the weeks that had passed since the tragedy her composure had been amazing.

Mr. Joyce shrugged his shoulders.

"The fact is, I suppose," he reflected, "that you can never tell what hidden possibilities of savagery there are in the most respectable of women."

There was a knock at the door.

"Come in."

The Chinese clerk entered and closed the door behind him. He closed it gently, with deliberation, but decidedly, and advanced to the table at which Mr. Joyce was sitting.

"May I trouble you, sir, for a few words' private conversation?" he said.

The elaborate accuracy with which the clerk expressed himself always faintly amused Mr. Joyce, and now he smiled.

"It's no trouble, Chi Seng," he replied.

"The matter on which I desire to speak to you, sir, is delicate and confidential."

"Fire away."

Mr. Joyce met his clerk's shrewd eyes. As usual Ong Chi Seng was dressed in the height of local fashion. He wore very shiny patent-leather shoes and gay silk socks. In his black tie was a pearl and ruby pin, and on the fourth finger of his left hand a diamond ring. From the pocket of his neat white coat protruded a gold fountain pen and a gold pencil. He wore a gold wrist-watch, and on the bridge of his nose invisible pince-nez. He gave a little cough.

"The matter has to do with the case R. v. Crosbie, sir."

"Yes?"

"A circumstance has come to my knowledge, sir, which seems to me to put a different complexion on it."

"What circumstance?"

"It has come to my knowledge, sir, that there is a letter in existence from the defendant to the unfortunate victim of the tragedy."

"I shouldn't be at all surprised. In the course of the last seven years I have no doubt that Mrs. Crosbie often had occasion to write to Mr. Hammond."

Mr. Joyce had a high opinion of his clerk's intelligence and his words were designed to conceal his thoughts.

"That is very probable, sir. Mrs. Crosbie must have communicated with the deceased frequently, to invite him to dine with her for example, or to propose a tennis game. That was my first thought when the matter was brought to my notice. This letter, however, was written on the day of the late Mr. Hammond's death."

Mr. Joyce did not flicker an eyelash. He continued to look at Ong Chi Seng with the smile of faint amusement with which he generally talked to him.

"Who has told you this?"

"The circumstances were brought to my knowledge, sir, by a friend of mine."

Mr. Joyce knew better than to insist.

"You will no doubt recall, sir, that Mrs. Crosbie has stated that until the fatal night she had had no communication with the deceased for several weeks."

"Have you got the letter?"

"No, sir."

"What are its contents?"

"My fliend gave me a copy. Would you like to peruse it, sir?"

"I should."

Ong Chi Seng took from an inside pocket a bulky wallet. It was filled with papers, Singapore dollar notes and cigarette cards. From the confusion he presently extracted a half sheet of thin note-paper and placed it before Mr. Joyce. The letter read as follows:

> R. *will be away for the night. I absolutely must see you. I shall expect you at eleven. I am desperate and if you don't come I won't answer for the consequences. Don't drive up.—L.*

It was written in the flowing hand which the Chinese were taught at the foreign schools. The writing, so lacking in character, was oddly incongruous with the ominous words.

"What makes you think that this note was written by Mrs. Crosbie?"

"I have every confidence in the veracity of my informant, sir," replied Ong Chi Seng. "And the matter can very easily be put to the proof. Mrs. Crosbie will no doubt be able to tell you at once whether she wrote such a letter or not."

Since the beginning of the conversation Mr. Joyce had not taken his eyes off the respectful countenance of his clerk. He wondered now if he discerned in it a faint expression of mockery.

"It is inconceivable that Mrs. Crosbie should have written such a letter," said Mr. Joyce.

"If that is your opinion, sir, the matter is of course ended. My fliend spoke to me on the subject only because he thought, as I was in your office, you might like to know of the existence of this letter before a communication was made to the Deputy Public Prosecutor."

"Who has the original?" asked Mr. Joyce sharply.

Ong Chi Seng made no sign that he perceived in this question and its manner a change of attitude.

"You will remember, sir, no doubt, that after the death of Mr. Hammond it was discovered that he had had relations with a Chinese woman. The letter is at present in her possession."

That was one of the things which had turned

public opinion most vehemently against Hammond. It came to be known that for several months he had had a Chinese woman living in his house.

For a moment neither of them spoke. Indeed everything had been said and each understood the other perfectly.

"I'm obliged to you, Chi Seng. I will give the matter my consideration."

"Very good, sir. Do you wish me to make a communication to that effect to my friend?"

"I daresay it would be as well if you kept in touch with him," Mr. Joyce answered with gravity.

"Yes, sir."

The clerk noiselessly left the room, shutting the door again with deliberation, and left Mr. Joyce to his reflections. He stared at the copy, in its neat, impersonal writing, of Leslie's letter. Vague suspicions troubled him. They were so disconcerting that he made an effort to put them out of his mind. There must be a simple explanation of the letter, and Leslie without doubt could give it at once, but, by heaven, an explanation was needed. He rose from his chair, put the letter in his pocket, and took his topee. When he went out Ong Chi Seng was busily writing at his desk.

"I'm going out for a few minutes, Chi Seng," he said.

"Mr. George Reed is coming by appointment at twelve o'clock, sir. Where shall I say you've gone?"

Mr. Joyce gave him a thin smile.

"You can say that you haven't the least idea."

But he knew perfectly well that Ong Chi Seng was aware that he was going to the jail. Though the crime had been committed in Belanda and the trial was to take place at Belanda Bharu, since there was in the jail there no convenience for the detention of a white woman Mrs. Crosbie had been brought to Singapore.

When she was led into the room in which he waited she held out her thin, distinguished hand, and gave him a pleasant smile. She was as ever neatly and simply dressed and her abundant, pale hair was arranged with care.

"I wasn't expecting to see you this morning," she said graciously.

She might have been in her own house, and Mr. Joyce almost expected to hear her call the boy and tell him to bring the visitor a gin pahit.

"How are you?" he asked.

"I'm in the best of health, thank you." A flicker of amusement flashed across her eyes. "This is a wonderful place for a rest cure."

The attendant withdrew and they were left alone.

"Do sit down," said Leslie.

He took a chair. He did not quite know how to begin. She was so cool that it seemed almost impossible to say to her the thing he had come to say. Though she was not pretty there was something agreeable in her appearance. She had elegance, but it was the elegance of good breeding in which there was nothing of the artifice of society. You had only to look at her to know what sort of people she had and what kind of surroundings she had lived in. Her fragility gave her a singular refinement. It was impossible to associate her with the vaguest idea of grossness.

"I'm looking forward to seeing Robert this afternoon," she said, in her good-humoured, easy voice. (It was a pleasure to hear her speak, her voice and her accent were so distinctive of her class.) "Poor dear, it's been a great trial to his nerves. I'm thankful it'll all be over in a few days."

"It's only five days now."

"I know. Each morning when I awake I say to myself, 'one less.'" She smiled then. "Just as I used to do at school and the holidays were coming."

"By the way, am I right in thinking that you had no communication whatever with Hammond for several weeks before the catastrophe?"

"I'm quite positive of that. The last time we met was at a tennis-party at the MacFarrens'. I don't think I said more than two words to him. They have two courts, you know, and we didn't happen to be in the same sets."

"And you haven't written to him?"

"Oh, no."

"Are you quite sure of that?"

"Oh, quite," she answered, with a little smile. "There was nothing I should write to him for except to ask him to dine or to play tennis, and I hadn't done either for months."

"At one time you'd been on fairly intimate terms with him. How did it happen that you had stopped asking him to anything?"

Mrs. Crosbie shrugged her thin shoulders.

"One gets tired of people. We hadn't anything very much in common. Of course, when he was ill Robert and I did everything we could for him, but the last year or two he'd been quite well, and he was very popular. He had a good many calls on his time, and there didn't seem to be any need to shower invitations upon him."

"Are you quite certain that was all?"

Mrs. Crosbie hesitated for a moment.

"Well, I may just as well tell you. It had come to our ears that he was living with a Chinese woman, and Robert said he wouldn't have him in the house. I had seen her myself."

Mr. Joyce was sitting in a straight-backed arm-chair, resting his chin on his hand, and his eyes were fixed on Leslie. Was it his fancy that as she made this remark her black pupils were filled on a sudden, for the fraction of a second, with a dull red light? The effect was startling. Mr. Joyce shifted in his chair. He placed the tips of his ten fingers together. He spoke very slowly, choosing his words.

"I think I should tell you that there is in existence a letter in your handwriting to Geoff. Hammond."

He watched her closely. She made no movement, nor did her face change colour, but she took a notice-able time to reply.

"In the past I've often sent him little notes to ask him to something or other, or to get me something when I knew he was going to Singapore."

"This letter asks him to come and see you because Robert was going to Singapore."

"That's impossible. I never did anything of the kind."

"You'd better read it for yourself."

He took it out of his pocket and handed it to her. She gave it a glance and with a smile of scorn handed it back to him.

"That's not my handwriting."

"I know, it's said to be an exact copy of the original."

She read the words now, and as she read a horrible change came over her. Her colourless face grew dreadful to look at. It turned green. The flesh seemed on a sudden to fall away and her skin was tightly stretched over the bones. Her lips receded, showing her teeth, so that she had the appearance of making a grimace. She stared at Mr. Joyce with eyes that started from their sockets. He was looking now at a gibbering death's head.

"What does it mean?" she whispered.

Her mouth was so dry that she could utter no more than a hoarse sound. It was no longer a human voice.

"That is for you to say," he answered.

"I didn't write it. I swear I didn't write it."

"Be very careful what you say. If the original is in your handwriting it would be useless to deny it."

"It would be a forgery."

"It would be difficult to prove that. It would be easy to prove that it was genuine."

A shiver passed through her lean body. But great beads of sweat stood on her forehead. She took a handkerchief from her bag and wiped the palms of her hands. She glanced at the letter again and gave Mr. Joyce a sidelong look.

"It's not dated. If I had written it and forgotten all about it, it might have been written years ago. If you'll give me time, I'll try and remember the circumstances."

"I noticed there was no date. If this letter were in the hands of the prosecution they would cross-examine the boys. They would soon find out whether some one took a letter to Hammond on the day of his death."

Mrs. Crosbie clasped her hands violently and swayed in her chair so that he thought she would faint.

"I swear to you that I didn't write that letter."

Mr. Joyce was silent for a little while. He took his eyes from her distraught face, and looked down on the floor. He was reflecting.

"In these circumstances we need not go into the matter further," he said slowly, at last breaking the silence. "If the possessor of this letter sees fit to place it in the hands of the prosecution you will be prepared."

His words suggested that he had nothing more to say to her, but he made no movement of departure. He waited. To himself he seemed to wait a very long time. He did not look at Leslie, but he was conscious that she sat very still. She made no sound. At last it was he who spoke.

"If you have nothing more to say to me I think I'll be getting back to my office."

"What would any one who read the letter be inclined to think that it meant?" she asked then.

"He'd know that you had told a deliberate lie," answered Mr. Joyce sharply.

"When?"

"You have stated definitely that you had had no communication with Hammond for at least three months."

"The whole thing has been a terrible shock to me. The events of that dreadful night have been a nightmare. It's not very strange if one detail has escaped my memory."

"It would be very unfortunate when your memory has reproduced so exactly every particular of your interview with Hammond, that you should have forgotten so important a point as that he came to see you in the bungalow on the night of his death at your express desire."

"I hadn't forgotten. After what happened I was afraid to mention it. I thought you'd none of you believe my story if I admitted that he'd come at my invitation. I daresay it was stupid of me; but I lost my head, and after I'd said once that I'd had no communication with Hammond I was obliged to stick to it."

By now Leslie had recovered her admirable composure, and she met Mr. Joyce's appraising glance with candour. Her gentleness was very disarming.

"You will be required to explain, then, *why* you asked Hammond to come and see you when Robert was away for the night."

She turned her eyes full on the lawyer. He had

been mistaken in thinking them insignificant, they were rather fine eyes, and unless he was mistaken they were bright now with tears. Her voice had a little break in it.

"It was a surprise I was preparing for Robert. His birthday is next month. I knew he wanted a new gun and you know I'm dreadfully stupid about sporting things. I wanted to talk to Geoff. about it. I thought I'd get him to order it for me."

"Perhaps the terms of the letter are not very clear to your recollection. Will you have another look at it?"

"No, I don't want to," she said quickly.

"Does it seem to you the sort of letter a woman would write to a somewhat distant acquaintance because she wanted to consult him about buying a gun?"

"I daresay it's rather extravagant and emotional. I do express myself like that, you know. I'm quite prepared to admit it's very silly." She smiled. "And after all, Geoff. Hammond wasn't quite a distant acquaintance. When he was ill I'd nursed him like a mother. I asked him to come when Robert was away, because Robert wouldn't have him in the house."

Mr. Joyce was tired of sitting so long in the same position. He rose and walked once or twice up and down the room, choosing the words he proposed to say; then he leaned over the back of the chair in which he had been sitting. He spoke slowly in a tone of deep gravity.

"Mrs. Crosbie, I want to talk to you very, very

seriously. This case was comparatively plain sailing. There was only one point which seemed to me to require explanation: as far as I could judge, you had fired no less than four shots into Hammond when he was lying on the ground. It was hard to accept the possibility that a delicate, frightened, and habitually self-controlled woman, of gentle nurture and refined instincts, should have surrendered to an absolutely uncontrolled frenzy. But of course it was admissible. Although Geoffrey Hammond was much liked and on the whole thought highly of, I was prepared to prove that he was the sort of man who might be guilty of the crime which in justification of your act you accused him of. The fact, which was discovered after his death, that he had been living with a Chinese woman gave us something very definite to go upon. That robbed him of any sympathy which might have been felt for him. We made up our minds to make use of the odium which such a connection cast upon him in the minds of all respectable people. I told your husband this morning that I was certain of an acquittal, and I wasn't just telling him that to give him heart. I do not believe the assessors would have left the court."

They looked into one another's eyes. Mrs. Crosbie was strangely still. She was like a little bird paralysed by the fascination of a snake. He went on in the same quiet tones.

"But this letter has thrown an entirely different complexion on the case. I am your legal adviser, I shall represent you in Court. I take your story as you tell it me, and I shall conduct your defence according to its terms. It may be that I believe your statements, and it may be that I doubt them. The duty of counsel is to persuade the Court that the evidence placed before it is not such as to justify it in bringing in a verdict of guilty, and any private opinion he may have of the guilt or innocence of his client is entirely beside the point."

He was astonished to see in Leslie's eyes the flicker of a smile. Piqued, he went on somewhat dryly.

"You're not going to deny that Hammond came to your house at your urgent, and I may even say, hysterical, invitation?"

Mrs. Crosbie, hesitating for an instant, seemed to consider.

"They can prove that the letter was taken to his bungalow by one of the house-boys. He rode over on his bicycle."

"You mustn't expect other people to be stupider than you. The letter will put them on the track of suspicions which have entered nobody's head. I will not tell you what I personally thought when I saw the copy. I do not wish you to tell me anything but what is needed to save your neck."

Mrs. Crosbie gave a shrill cry. She sprang to her feet, white with terror.

"You don't think they'd hang me?"

"If they came to the conclusion that you hadn't killed Hammond in self-defence, it would be the duty of the assessors to bring in a verdict of guilty. The charge is murder. It would be the duty of the judge to sentence you to death."

"But what can they prove?" she gasped.

"I don't know what they can prove. You know. I don't want to know. But if their suspicions are aroused, if they begin to make enquiries, if the natives are questioned—what is it that can be discovered?"

She crumpled up suddenly. She fell on the floor before he could catch her. She had fainted. He looked round the room for water, but there was none there, and he did not want to be disturbed. He stretched her out on the floor and kneeling beside her waited for her to recover. When she opened her eyes he was disconcerted by the ghastly fear that he saw in them.

"Keep quite still," he said. "You'll be better in a moment."

"You won't let them hang me," she whispered.

She began to cry, hysterically, while in undertones he sought to quieten her.

"For goodness' sake, pull yourself together," he said.

"Give me a minute."

Her courage was amazing. He could see the effort she made to regain her self-control, and soon she was once more calm.

"Let me get up now."

He gave her his hand and helped her to her feet. Taking her arm, he led her to the chair. She sat down wearily.

"Don't talk to me for a minute or two," she said.

"Very well."

When at last she spoke it was to say something which he did not expect. She gave a little sigh.

"I'm afraid I've made rather a mess of things," she said.

He did not answer, and once more there was a silence.

"Isn't it possible to get hold of the letter?" she said at last.

"I do not think anything would have been said to me about it if the person in whose possession it is was not prepared to sell it."

"Who's got it?"

"The Chinese woman who was living in Hammond's house."

A spot of colour flickered for an instant on Leslie's cheek-bones.

"Does she want an awful lot for it?"

"I imagine that she has a very shrewd idea of its value. I doubt if it would be possible to get hold of it except for a very large sum."

"Are you going to let me be hanged?"

"Do you think it's so simple as all that to secure possession of an unwelcome piece of evidence? It's no different from suborning a witness. You have no right to make any such suggestion to me."

"Then what is going to happen to me?"

"Justice must take its course."

She grew very pale. A little shudder passed through her body.

"I put myself in your hands. Of course I have no right to ask you to do anything that isn't proper."

Mr. Joyce had not bargained for the little break in her voice which her habitual self-restraint made quite intolerably moving. She looked at him with humble eyes and he thought that if he rejected their appeal they would haunt him for the rest of his life. After all, nothing could bring poor Hammond back to life again. He wondered what really was the explanation of that letter. It was not fair to conclude from it that she had killed Hammond without provocation. He had lived in the East a long time and his sense of professional honour was not perhaps so acute as it had been twenty years before. He stared at the floor. He made up his mind to do something which he knew was unjustifiable, but it stuck in his throat and he felt dully resentful towards Leslie. It embarrassed him a little to speak.

"I don't know exactly what your husband's circumstances are?"

Flushing a rosy red, she shot a swift glance at him.

"He has a good many tin shares and a small share in two or three rubber estates. I suppose he could raise money."

"He would have to be told what it was for."

She was silent for a moment. She seemed to think.

"He's in love with me still. He would make any sacrifice to save me. Is there any need for him to see the letter?"

Mr. Joyce frowned a little, and, quick to notice, she went on.

"Robert is an old friend of yours. I'm not asking you to do anything for me, I'm asking you to save a rather simple, kind man who never did you any harm from all the pain that's possible."

Mr. Joyce did not reply. He rose to go and Mrs. Crosbie, with the grace that was natural to her, held out her hand. She was shaken by the scene, and her look was haggard, but she made a brave attempt to speed him with courtesy.

"It's so good of you to take all this trouble for me. I can't begin to tell you how grateful I am."

Mr. Joyce returned to his office. He sat in his own room, quite still, attempting to do no work, and pondered. His imagination brought him many strange ideas. He shuddered a little. At last there was the discreet knock on the door which he was expecting. Ong Chi Seng came in.

"I was just going out to have my tiffin, sir," he said.

"All right."

"I didn't know if there was anything you wanted before I went, sir."

"I don't think so. Did you make another appointment for Mr. Reed?"

"Yes, sir. He will come at three o'clock."

"Good."

Ong Chi Seng turned away, walked to the door, and put his long slim fingers on the handle. Then, as though on an afterthought, he turned back.

"Is there anything you wish me to say to my fliend, sir?"

Although Ong Chi Seng spoke English so admirably he had still a difficulty with the letter r, and he pronounced it "fliend."

"What friend?"

"About the letter Mrs. Crosbie wrote to Hammond deceased, sir."

"Oh! I'd forgotten about that. I mentioned it to Mrs. Crosbie and she denies having written anything of the sort. It's evidently a forgery."

Mr. Joyce took the copy from his pocket and handed it to Ong Chi Seng. Ong Chi Seng ignored the gesture.

"In that case, sir, I suppose there would be no objection if my fliend delivered the letter to the Deputy Public Prosecutor."

"None. But I don't quite see what good that would do your friend."

"My fliend, sir, thought it was his duty in the interests of justice."

"I am the last man in the world to interfere with any one who wishes to do his duty, Chi Seng."

The eyes of the lawyer and of the Chinese clerk met. Not the shadow of a smile hovered on the lips of either, but they understood each other perfectly.

"I quite understand, sir," said Ong Chi Seng, "but from my study of the case R. v. Crosbie I am of opinion that the production of such a letter would be damaging to our client."

"I have always had a very high opinion of your legal acumen, Chi Seng."

"It has occurred to me, sir, that if I could persuade my fliend to induce the Chinese woman who has the letter to deliver it into our hands it would save a great deal of trouble."

Mr. Joyce idly drew faces on his blotting-paper.

"I suppose your friend is a business man. In what circumstances do you think he would be induced to part with the letter?"

"He has not got the letter. The Chinese woman has the letter. He is only a relation of the Chinese woman. She is an ignorant woman; she did not know the value of the letter till my fliend told her."

"What value did he put on it?"

"Ten thousand dollars, sir."

"Good God! Where on earth do you suppose Mrs. Crosbie can get ten thousand dollars! I tell you the letter's a forgery."

He looked up at Ong Chi Seng as he spoke. The clerk was unmoved by the outburst. He stood at the side of the desk, civil, cool and observant.

"Mr. Crosbie owns an eighth share of the Betong Rubber Estate and a sixth share of the Selantan River Rubber Estate. I have a fliend who will lend him the money on the security of his properties."

"You have a large circle of acquaintance, Chi Seng."

"Yes, sir."

"Well, you can tell them to go to hell. I would nevei advise Mr. Crosbie to give a penny more than five thousand for a letter that can be very easily explained."

"The Chinese woman does not want to sell the letter, sir. My fliend took a long time to persuade her. It is useless to offer her less than the sum mentioned."

Mr. Joyce looked at Ong Chi Seng for at least three minutes. The clerk bore the searching scrutiny without embarrassment. He stood in a respectful attitude with downcast eyes. Mr. Joyce knew his man. Clever fellow, Chi Seng, he thought, I wonder how much he's going to get out of it.

"Ten thousand dollars is a very large sum."

"Mr. Crosbie will certainly pay it rather than see his wife hanged, sir."

Again Mr. Joyce paused. What more did Chi Seng know than he had said? He must be pretty sure of his ground if he was obviously so unwilling to bargain. That sum had been fixed because whoever it was that was managing the affair knew it was the largest amount that Robert Crosbie could raise.

"Where is the Chinese woman now?" asked Mr. Joyce.

"She is staying at the house of my fliend, sir."

"Will she come here?"

"I think it more better if you go to her, sir. I can take you to the house to-night and she will give you the letter. She is a very ignorant woman, sir, and she does not understand cheques."

"I wasn't thinking of giving her a cheque. I will bring banknotes with me."

"It would only be waste of valuable time to bring less than ten thousand dollars, sir."

"I quite understand."

"I will go and tell my fliend after I have had my tiffin, sir."

"Very good. You'd better meet me outside the club at ten o'clock to-night."

"With pleasure, sir," said Ong Chi Seng.

He gave Mr. Joyce a little bow and left the room. Mr. Joyce went out to have luncheon too. He went to the club and here, as he had expected, he saw Robert Crosbie. He was sitting at a crowded table, and as he passed him, looking for a place, Mr. Joyce touched him on the shoulder.

"I'd like a word or two with you before you go," he said.

"Right you are. Let me know when you're ready."

Mr. Joyce had made up his mind how to tackle him. He played a rubber of bridge after luncheon in order to allow time for the club to empty itself. He did not want on this particular matter to see Crosbie in his office. Presently Crosbie came into the card-room and looked on till the game was finished. The other players went on their various affairs, and the two were left alone.

"A rather unfortunate thing has happened, old man," said Mr. Joyce, in a tone which he sought to render as casual as possible. "It appears that your wife sent a letter to Hammond asking him to come to the bungalow on the night he was killed."

"But that's impossible," cried Crosbie. "She's always stated that she had had no communication with Hammond. I know from my own knowledge that she hadn't set eyes on him for a couple of months."

"The fact remains that the letter exists. It's in the possession of the Chinese woman Hammond was living with. Your wife meant to give you a present on your birthday, and she wanted Hammond to help her to get it. In the emotional excitement that she suffered from after the tragedy, she forgot all about it, and having once denied having any com-

munication with Hammond, she was afraid to say
that she had made a mistake. It was of course very
unfortunate, but I daresay it was not unnatural."

Crosbie did not speak. His large, red face bore
an expression of complete bewilderment, and Mr.
Joyce was at once relieved and exasperated by his
lack of comprehension. He was a stupid man, and
Mr. Joyce had no patience with stupidity. But his
distress since the catastrophe had touched a soft
spot in the lawyer's heart; and Mrs. Crosbie had
struck the right note when she asked him to help her,
not for her sake, but for her husband's.

"I need not tell you that it would be very awkward if this letter found its way into the hands of
the prosecution. Your wife has lied, and she would
be asked to explain the lie. It alters things a little
if Hammond did not intrude, an unwanted guest,
but came to your house by invitation. It would be
easy to arouse in the assessors a certain indecision of
mind."

Mr. Joyce hesitated. He was face to face now
with his decision. If it had been a time for humour,
he could have smiled at the reflection that he was
taking so grave a step, and that the man for whom
he was taking it had not the smallest conception of
its gravity. If he gave the matter a thought, he
probably imagined that what Mr. Joyce was doing
was what any lawyer did in the ordinary run of business.

"My dear Robert, you are not only my client, but
my friend. I think we must get hold of that letter.
It'll cost a good deal of money. Except for that I

should have preferred to say nothing to you about it."

"How much?"

"Ten thousand dollars."

"That's a devil of a lot. With the slump and one thing and another it'll take just about all I've got."

"Can you get it at once?"

"I suppose so. Old Charlie Meadows will let me have it on my tin shares and on those two estates I'm interested in."

"Then will you?"

"Is it absolutely necessary?"

"If you want your wife to be acquitted."

Crosbie grew very red. His mouth sagged strangely.

"But . . ." He could not find words, his face now was purple. "But I don't understand. She can explain. You don't mean to say they'd find her guilty? They couldn't hang her for putting a noxious vermin out of the way."

"Of course they wouldn't hang her. They might only find her guilty of manslaughter. She'd probably get off with two or three years."

Crosbie started to his feet and his red face was distraught with horror.

"Three years."

Then something seemed to dawn in that slow intelligence of his. His mind was darkness across which shot suddenly a flash of lightning, and though the succeeding darkness was as profound, there remained the memory of something not seen but perhaps just descried. Mr. Joyce saw that Crosbie's big red hands, coarse and hard with all the odd jobs he had set them to, trembled.

"What was the present she wanted to make me?"

"She says she wanted to give you a new gun."

Once more that great red face flushed a deeper red.

"When have you got to have the money ready?"

There was something odd in his voice now. It sounded as though he spoke with invisible hands clutching at his throat.

"At ten o'clock to-night. I thought you could bring it to my office at about six."

"Is the woman coming to you?"

"No, I'm going to her."

"I'll bring the money. I'll come with you."

Mr. Joyce looked at him sharply.

"Do you think there's any need for you to do that? I think it would be better if you left me to deal with this matter by myself."

"It's my money, isn't it? I'm going to come."

Mr. Joyce shrugged his shoulders. They rose and shook hands. Mr. Joyce looked at him curiously.

At ten o'clock they met in the empty club.

"Everything all right?" asked Mr. Joyce.

"Yes. I've got the money in my pocket."

"Let's go then."

They walked down the steps. Mr. Joyce's car was waiting for them in the square, silent at that hour, and as they came to it Ong Chi Seng stepped out of the shadow of a house. He took his seat beside the driver and gave him a direction. They drove past the Hotel de l'Europe and turned up by the Sailors' Home to get into Victoria Street. Here the Chinese shops were open still, idlers lounged about, and in the roadway rickshaws and motor-cars and gharries gave a busy air to the scene. Suddenly their car stopped and Chi Seng turned round.

"I think it more better if we walk here, sir," he said.

They got out and he went on. They followed a step or two behind. Then he asked them to stop.

"You wait here, sir. I go in and speak to my fliend."

He went into a shop, open to the street, where three or four Chinese were standing behind the counter. It was one of those strange shops where nothing was on view and you wondered what it was they sold there. They saw him address a stout man in a duck suit with a large gold chain across his breast and the man shot a quick glance out into the night. He gave Chi Seng a key and Chi Seng came out. He beckoned to the two men waiting and slid into a doorway at the side of the shop. They followed him and found themselves at the foot of a flight of stairs.

"If you wait a minute I will light a match," he said, always resourceful. "You come upstairs, please."

He held a Japanese match in front of them, but it scarcely dispelled the darkness and they groped their way up behind him. On the first floor he unlocked a door and going in lit a gas-jet.

"Come in, please," he said.

It was a small square room, with one window, and the only furniture consisted of two low Chinese beds covered with matting. In one corner was a large chest, with an elaborate lock, and on this stood a shabby tray with an opium pipe on it and a lamp. There was in the room the faint, acrid scent of the drug. They sat down and Ong Chi Seng offered them cigarettes. In a moment the door was opened by the fat Chinaman whom they had seen behind the counter. He bade them good evening in very good English and sat down by the side of his fellow-countryman.

"The Chinese woman is just coming," said Chi Seng.

A boy from the shop brought in a tray with a teapot and cups and the Chinaman offered them a cup of tea. Crosbie refused. The Chinese talked to one another in undertones, but Crosbie and Mr. Joyce were silent. At last there was the sound of a voice outside; some one was calling in a low tone; and the Chinaman went to the door. He opened it, spoke a few words, and ushered a woman in. Mr. Joyce looked at her. He had heard much about her since Hammond's death, but he had never seen her. She was a stoutish person, not very young, with a broad, phlegmatic face. She was powdered and rouged and her eyebrows were a thin black line, but she gave you the impression of a woman of character. She wore a pale blue jacket and a white skirt, her costume was not quite European nor quite Chinese, but on her feet were little Chinese silk slippers. She wore heavy gold chains round her neck, gold bangles on her wrists, gold ear-rings and elaborate gold pins in her black hair. She walked in slowly, with the air of a woman sure of herself, but with a certain heaviness of tread, and sat down on the bed beside Ong Chi Seng. He said something to her and nodding she gave an incurious glance at the two white men.

"Has she got the letter?" asked Mr. Joyce.

"Yes, sir."

Crosbie said nothing, but produced a roll of five-hundred-dollar notes. He counted out twenty and handed them to Chi Seng.

"Will you see if that is correct?"

The clerk counted them and gave them to the fat Chinaman.

"Quite correct, sir."

The Chinaman counted them once more and put them in his pocket. He spoke again to the woman and she drew from her bosom a letter. She gave it to Chi Seng who cast his eyes over it.

"This is the right document, sir," he said, and was about to give it to Mr. Joyce when Crosbie took it from him.

"Let me look at it," he said.

Mr. Joyce watched him read and then held out his hand for it.

"You'd better let me have it."

Crosbie folded it up deliberately and put it in his pocket.

"No, I'm going to keep it myself. It's cost me enough money."

Mr. Joyce made no rejoinder. The three Chinese watched the little passage, but what they thought about it, or whether they thought, it was impossible to tell from their impassive countenances. Mr. Joyce rose to his feet.

"Do you want me any more to-night, sir?" said Ong Chi Seng.

"No." He knew that the clerk wished to stay behind in order to get his agreed share of the money, and he turned to Crosbie. "Are you ready?"

Crosbie did not answer, but stood up. The Chinaman went to the door and opened it for them. Chi Seng found a bit of candle and lit it in order to light them down, and the two Chinese accompanied them to the street. They left the woman sitting quietly on the bed smoking a cigarette. When they reached the street the Chinese left them and went once more upstairs.

"What are you going to do with that letter?" asked Mr. Joyce.

"Keep it."

They walked to where the car was waiting for them and here Mr. Joyce offered his friend a lift. Crosbie shook his head.

"I'm going to walk." He hesitated a little and shuffled his feet. "I went to Singapore on the night of Hammond's death partly to buy a new gun that a man I knew wanted to dispose of. Good night."

He disappeared quickly into the darkness.

Mr. Joyce was quite right about the trial. The assessors went into court fully determined to acquit Mrs. Crosbie. She gave evidence on her own behalf. She told her story simply and with straightforwardness. The D.P.P. was a kindly man and it was plain that he took no great pleasure in his task. He asked the necessary questions in a deprecating manner. His speech for the prosecution might really have been a speech for the defence, and the assessors took less than five minutes to consider their popular verdict. It was impossible to prevent the great outburst of applause with which it was received by the crowd that packed the court-house. The judge congratulated Mrs. Crosbie and she was a free woman.

No one had expressed a more violent disapprobation of Hammond's behaviour than Mrs. Joyce; she was a woman loyal to her friends and she had insisted on the Crosbies staying with her after the trial, for she in common with every one else had no doubt of the result, till they could make arrangements to go away. It was out of the question for poor, dear, brave Leslie to return to the bungalow at which the horrible catastrophe had taken place. The trial was over by half-past twelve and when they reached the Joyces' house a grand luncheon was awaiting them. Cocktails were ready, Mrs. Joyce's million-dollar cocktail was celebrated through all the Malay States, and Mrs. Joyce drank Leslie's health. She was a talkative, vivacious woman, and now she was in the highest spirits. It was fortunate, for the rest of them were silent. She did not wonder, her husband never had much to say, and the other two were naturally exhausted from the long strain to which they had been subjected. During luncheon she carried on a bright and spirited monologue. Then coffee was served.

"Now, children," she said in her gay, bustling

fashion, "you must have a rest and after tea I shall take you both for a drive to the sea."

Mr. Joyce, who lunched at home only by exception, had of course to go back to his office.

"I'm afraid I can't do that, Mrs. Joyce," said Crosbie. "I've got to get back to the estate at once."

"Not to-day?" she cried.

"Yes, now. I've neglected it for too long and I have urgent business. But I shall be very grateful if you will keep Leslie until we have decided what to do."

Mrs. Joyce was about to expostulate, but her husband prevented her.

"If he must go, he must, and there's an end of it."

There was something in the lawyer's tone which made her look at him quickly. She held her tongue and there was a moment's silence. Then Crosbie spoke again.

"If you'll forgive me, I'll start at once so that I can get there before dark." He rose from the table. "Will you come and see me off, Leslie?"

"Of course."

They went out of the dining-room together.

"I think that's rather inconsiderate of him," said Mrs. Joyce. "He must know that Leslie wants to be with him just now."

"I'm sure he wouldn't go if it wasn't absolutely necessary."

"Well, I'll just see that Leslie's room is ready for her. She wants a complete rest, of course, and then amusement."

Mrs. Joyce left the room and Joyce sat down again. In a short time he heard Crosbie start the engine of his motor-cycle and then noisily scrunch over the gravel of the garden path. He got up and went into the drawing-room. Mrs. Crosbie was standing in the middle of it, looking into space, and in her hand was an open letter. He recognised it. She gave him a glance as he came in and he saw that she was deathly pale.

"He knows," she whispered.

Mr. Joyce went up to her and took the letter from her hand. He lit a match and set the paper afire. She watched it burn. When he could hold it no longer he dropped it on the tiled floor and they both looked at the paper curl and blacken. Then he trod it into ashes with his foot.

"What does he know?"

She gave him a long, long stare and into her eyes came a strange look. Was it contempt or despair? Mr. Joyce could not tell.

"He knows that Geoff. was my lover."

Mr. Joyce made no movement and uttered no sound.

"He'd been my lover for years. He became my lover almost immediately after he came back from the war. We knew how careful we must be. When we became lovers I pretended I was tired of him, and he seldom came to the house when Robert was there. I used to drive out to a place we knew and he met me, two or three times a week, and when Robert went to Singapore he used to come to the bungalow late, when the boys had gone for the night. We saw

one another constantly, all the time, and not a soul
had the smallest suspicion of it. And then lately, a
year ago, he began to change. I didn't know what
was the matter. I couldn't believe that he didn't
care for me any more. He always denied it. I was
frantic. I made him scenes. Sometimes I thought
he hated me. Oh, if you knew what agonies I endured. I passed through hell. I knew he didn't
want me any more and I wouldn't let him go. Mis-
sery! Misery! I loved him. I'd given him everything. He was all my life. And then I heard he was
living with a Chinese woman. I couldn't believe it.
I wouldn't believe it. At last I saw her, I saw her
with my own eyes, walking in the village, with her
gold bracelets and her necklaces, an old, fat, Chinese
woman. She was older than I was. Horrible! They
all knew in the kampong that she was his mistress.
And when I passed her, she looked at me and I knew
that she knew I was his mistress too. I sent for him.
I told him I must see him. You've read the letter.
I was mad to write it. I didn't know what I was
doing. I didn't care. I hadn't seen him for ten days.
It was a lifetime. And when last we'd parted he
took me in his arms and kissed me and told me not
to worry. And he went straight from my arms to
hers."

She had been speaking in a low voice, vehemently,
and now she stopped and wrung her hands.

"That damned letter. We'd always been so careful. He always tore up any word I wrote to him the
moment he'd read it. How was I to know he'd leave
that one? He came and I told him I knew about the

Chinawoman. He denied it. He said it was only scandal. I was beside myself. I don't know what I said to him. Oh, I hated him then. I tore him limb from limb. I said everything I could to wound him. I insulted him. I could have spat in his face. And at last he turned on me. He told me he was sick and tired of me and never wanted to see me again. He said I bored him to death. And then he acknowledged that it was true about the Chinawoman. He said he'd known her for years, before the war, and she was the only woman who really meant anything to him, and the rest was just pastime. And he said he was glad I knew, and now at last I'd leave him alone. And then I don't know what happened, I was beside myself, I saw red. I seized the revolver and I fired. He gave a cry and I saw I'd hit him. He staggered and rushed for the verandah. I ran after him and fired again. He fell, and then I stood over him and I fired and fired till the revolver went click, click, and I knew there were no more cartridges."

At last she stopped, panting. Her face was no longer human, it was distorted with cruelty, and rage and pain. You would never have thought that this quiet, refined woman was capable of such a fiendish passion. Mr. Joyce took a step backwards. He was absolutely aghast at the sight of her. It was not a face, it was a gibbering, hideous mask. Then they heard a voice calling from another room, a loud, friendly, cheerful voice. It was Mrs. Joyce.

"Come along, Leslie darling, your room's ready. You must be dropping with sleep."

Mrs. Crosbie's features gradually composed themselves. Those passions, so clearly delineated, were smoothed away as with your hand you would smooth a crumpled paper, and in a minute the face was cool and calm and unlined. She was a trifle pale, but her lips broke into a pleasant, affable smile. She was once more the well-bred and even distinguished woman.

"I'm coming, Dorothy dear. I'm sorry to give you so much trouble."

POSTSCRIPT

With the exception of Singapore, a city too busy with its own concerns to bother itself with trifles, imaginary names have been chosen for the places in which the action of these stories is supposed to be conducted. Some of the smaller communities in the countries washed by the China Sea are very sensitive, and their members are much agitated if, in a work of fiction, a hint is given that the circumstances of their lives are not always such as would meet the approval of the suburban circles in which contentedly dwell their cousins and their aunts. It must indeed astonish the traveller to discover that the English who pass the best part of their lives in the spacious East attach so much importance to a Parish Pump, and he may even wonder at times that they are content to go so far afield as the Celebes only to find themselves in Bedford Park. Being practical people concerned for the most part with practical affairs they give the writer credit for little imagination and, knowing that he has been in this or that place and made the acquaintance of this or that person, jump to the conclusion that in the characters of his invention he has done no more than draw portraits of themselves.

Living, with all the East about them, as narrowly as in a market-town, they have the market-town's *faults and foibles; and seem to take a malicious pleasure in looking for the originals of the characters, especially if they are mean, foolish or vicious, which the author has chosen for the persons of his stories. They have small acquaintance with arts and letters and do not understand that the disposition and appearance of a person in a short story are dictated by the exigencies of the intrigue. Nor has it occurred to them that actual persons are much too shadowy to serve as characters in a work of the imagination. We see real people only in the flat, but for the purposes of fiction they must be seen in the round; and to make a living personage it is necessary to combine suggestions drawn from a dozen sources. Because a reader, unprofitably employing a useless leisure, recognises in a character one trait, mental or physical, of some one he knows and is aware the author has met, it is silly to put the name of this person to the character described and say: here is a portrait. A work of fiction, and perhaps I should not go too far if I spoke more generally and said a work of art, is an arrangement which the author makes of the facts of his experience with the idiosyncrasies of his own personality. It is an unlikely, and unimportant, accident if it happens to be a copy of life. So the Greek sculptor of a famous piece gave a woman six toes, because thus he thought doubtless to increase the slender elegance of her foot. Facts are but a canvas on which the artist draws a significant pattern. I venture therefore to claim that the persons of these stories are imaginary, but since an incident in one of them,* The Yellow

Streak, *was suggested by a misadventure of my own, I wish more particularly to state that no reference is intended to either of my companions on that hazardous occasion.*

THE END